RETURN TO MORMONVILLE:
WORLDS APART

RETURN TO MORMONVILLE:
WORLDS APART

by Jeff Call

CFI

Springville, Utah

ISBN: 1-55517-799-9
e.1

Published by CFI
Imprint of Cedar Fort Inc.
www.cedarfort.com

Distributed by:

Typeset by Natalie Roach
Cover design by Nicole Shaffer
Cover design © 2004 by Lyle Mortimer

Printed in the United States of America
10 9 8 7 6 5 4 3 2 1
Printed on acid-free paper

Library of Congress Cataloging-in-Publication Data

Call, Jeff, 1968-
    Return to Mormonville : worlds apart / by Jeff Call.-- 1st ed.
        p. cm.
    ISBN 1-55517-799-9 (alk. paper)
    1. Mormons--Fiction. 2. Utah--Fiction. I. Title.

    PS3603.A44R48 2004
    813'.6--dc22

2004022270

DEDICATION

To my wife CherRon, and my sons Ryan, Brayden, Landon, Austin, Carson, and Janson.

1

Standing before the assembled throng, Brother Munchak straightened his star-spangled tie, cracked his knuckles, and cheerily welcomed everyone to Sunday School. The glint of the American flag pin on his lapel momentarily blinded Sister Fidrych, who was sitting on the front row. A strategically placed briefcase, adorned with a "Munchak Munchies" sticker, sat on a table next to Brother Munchak.

He cast his eyes to the back row where Luke Manning was trying to hide behind 370-pound Brother Sagapolu.

"Brother Manning," Brother Munchak asked, "would you please offer the opening prayer for us?"

An unsavory word Luke had been trying to eliminate from his vocabulary briefly popped into his mind. He was proud of himself for not using profanity anymore, thanks to months of rehabilitation in the form of a swearing jar, but some curse words—a vestige of a former life—still presented themselves occasionally.

Fact was, Luke didn't feel like praying—he was hoping to sit back and catch a little nap. That morning, after all, he woke up at six to attend a stake general priesthood meeting, where he was called on to offer the closing prayer.

"You bet," Luke told Brother Munchak as he lifted his athletic frame off the cushioned chair and ambled to the front of the room. Luke was called on a lot to pray at church. He figured that everyone wanted him to make up for lost time.

Even though he had been a member of The Church of Jesus

Christ of Latter-day Saints for more than two years, Luke still felt self-conscious about saying prayers in public, especially in front of a room full of people who were life-long members of the Church. They were nice folks who came from solid Pioneer stock and could tell stories about a great-great-great-great-grand-something who had crossed the plains barefoot while pushing a handcart. Many of Luke's ancestors, on the other hand, were probably among those who forced the pioneers to flee their homes in the East.

Luke felt spiritually inferior to just about everybody in the ward, up to and including the Sunbeams. He was striving to be a worthy priesthood holder, but invariably he felt like he fell short—especially when he'd look at the other men in the ward, the vast majority of whom were returned missionaries and looked and acted like poster boys for the Mormon way of life. The trouble for Luke was, he wasn't perfect, but he belonged to a church that encouraged, promoted, and even demanded perfection.

Ward members were genuinely nice to Luke, but some treated him *too* nicely, almost condescendingly, as if he were the ward mascot or some Mormon urban legend. He overheard the whispers from time to time when visitors came to church.

"Look! That's him. Luke Manning. He came from New York City to write terrible things about the Church, but he ended up getting baptized. If that isn't the ultimate proof that the Church is true, I don't know what is . . ."

The gold plates weren't available, so he became Exhibit A. All in all, he felt more comfortable in Primary, where the kids simply liked to make fun of his New York accent.

While Luke took pride in his command of the English language, his prayers were somewhat stilted. Saying "thee," "thy," and "thou" didn't exactly roll off his tongue naturally, let alone conjugating "will" into "wilt."

Wilt—that's exactly what Luke felt like he was going to do as he prayed. Though the room was air-conditioned, he felt beads of sweat on his brow. At one point he paused, leaving a painfully awkward silence. After Luke abruptly closed his prayer,

Brother Munchak put his hands on Luke's shoulders, looked him in the eyes, and grinned. "Brother Manning, we sure do 'preciate ya," he said.

"Ditto," Luke replied.

Sunday School was always an adventure when Brother Munchak taught, kind of like Six Flags Over Temple Square. He liked working Ronald Reagan or Rush Limbaugh quotes into his lessons while extolling the virtues of the Republican Party. One time, during the lesson on Nephi's journey to the promised land, he asked Brother Chambliss to play *America the Beautiful* on the harmonica.

The previous week, for no particular or relevant reason, Brother Munchak claimed he had done his family's genealogy all the way back to Adam.

"Adam who?" Luke had asked Hayley, who playfully elbowed him in the ribs.

Luke never knew what Brother Munchak would say next, and that usually kept him interested.

"This week's lesson, Brothers and Sisters," Brother Munchak announced while scrawling something on the blackboard, "is on D&C 122. We're going to discuss trials and tribulation."

Except he misspelled the word "t-r-i-b-u-l-l-a-t-i-o-n."

Luke sat down next to Hayley, who smiled sweetly at him. He took that as a sign that he had done alright. She gently placed her left hand, on which she sported a diamond ring, on top of his right hand. Luke looked at the ring and compared it to the wedding band on his left hand. At first, he hadn't been sure about having to wear a ring all the time, but it had gotten to the point that he felt uncomfortable, almost lost, without it.

Most of the time, he couldn't believe that he was married to a woman as perfect as Hayley. Okay, maybe she wasn't perfect, but she was perfect for him. Every once in a while, he would have a recurring dream where a pair of men dressed in brown UPS uniforms would show up on his doorstep and announce, "Boy, did we make a mistake. We delivered this one to the wrong address!" And then they'd take her away. As far as Luke was concerned, the message was clear: he didn't deserve someone as special as Hayley. Then he'd wake up and he'd look over and she would be sleeping. For the next hour, he'd just lay there and ponder the incredulous events over the previous couple of years that had transpired and led him to her. He'd say a little prayer of gratitude, and then just watch her breathe before he'd fall asleep again. Luke was well aware that Hayley could have married a man who had been born-and-raised LDS, with "Eagle Scout," "seminary graduate," and "returned missionary" on his resume. Luke struggled to convince himself that he was worthy of her.

In general, Luke was happier than he'd ever dreamed possible. He had a new perspective on life—an eternal perspective. He was proud to be a member of the Church. Since his baptism, he had read *Mormon Doctrine* and *A Marvelous Work and a Wonder*. He got halfway through *The Miracle of Forgiveness* before he started getting an ulcer. The doctor advised him to find some new reading material.

Hayley sensed Luke's lack of confidence when it came to doctrinal knowledge, so every once in a while she would unpack her old seminary manuals and missionary discussion pamphlets and they'd study gospel subjects. She even had him memorize seminary mastery scriptures. She kept Luke in line. During sacrament meeting that morning, she noticed he had his eyes closed for quite some time.

"Luke," Hayley whispered, nudging him. "Wake up."

"I'm not sleeping," he said, "I'm, um, meditating."

"Do you usually snore when you meditate?"

Back in Sunday School, Luke noticed Brother Munchak's misspelling on the blackboard and it was eating at him. "I've got to say something," he whispered to Hayley. "It's hurting my eyes."

"I'm going to give you a piece of advice Lot gave to his wife," Hayley whispered back. "Just don't look at it."

"This is different," Luke said. "Don't worry. I'll do it tactfully."

Hayley shook her head and scrunched down in her seat.

Luke raised his hand and Brother Munchak stopped in mid-sentence. "Brother Manning, do you have a question or a comment?"

"It's no big deal, really, but you spelled tribulation with a double 'L'," Luke said.

"Excuse me?" Brother Munchak answered, staring at the blackboard.

"With all due respect, Brother Munchak," Luke said, "get the extra 'L' outta there."

Sister Fidrych gasped. Most of the class members laughed. Hayley turned a deep shade of red.

Brother Munchak laughed louder than anyone. "Spelling was never one of my strong suits," he said, erasing the extra letter. "Brother Manning, we can always count on you to add some levity to our class, not to mention some spelling tips. Thank you."

"Don't mention it," Luke replied.

"The scriptures are very clear that we can expect to have opposition in all things in the Last Days," Brother Munchak continued in a very scholarly fashion. "Turn with me to the Doctrine and Covenants, where we read prophecies about the wars, turmoil, and wickedness that will abound in the world during that period of time."

Luke removed his scriptures from under his chair. He looked over at Hayley and he was relieved to see that she was smiling again. The last thing he wanted to do was make her upset.

When Luke had lived in New York City, marriage had been the furthest thing from his mind. It seemed so confining, so constricting. He gradually realized it was just one of many things that had been missing from his life.

The temple ceremony that sealed Luke to Hayley for eternity instantly became the most cherished event in his life. Until he became a member of the Church, he had seen only two kinds of weddings: the soap opera wedding with all its pomp and circumstance, and the cheap Las Vegas style wedding. The one he experienced with Hayley in the Salt Lake Temple was different. It was the simplicity, and the profundity of it that left a lasting impression on him.

He only wished his mother could have been alive to see it.

Sheila Manning had come to Utah with Luke still a little

5

skeptical of the Mormons, but she was baptized not long after moving to Helaman. She was called to the Relief Society's compassionate service committee, and then, within a couple of days, she was diagnosed with lung cancer. Twenty years of smoking had caught up with her and she was gone within a couple of months. As sad as it was, Luke was grateful to the Lord for the chance he'd had to be reunited with her, if only for a little while, after years of estrangement. He looked forward to being reunited with her again someday—permanently.

Brother Munchak, meanwhile, was working up a sweat. He removed his jacket and placed it on the table. With his hands resting on his suspenders, he began preaching that the Second Coming was "nigh at hand." That gave him a perfect opportunity to shamelessly plug his food storage/emergency preparedness business. Brother Munchak referred to it as multi-level marketing.

Luke insisted it was a pyramid scheme, but he kept his views to himself.

"I'm not advocating this, of course, Brothers and Sisters," Brother Munchak said, "but our family has stockpiled enough food for two years and we've thrown in duct tape, gas masks, and chemical suits for good measure. As wicked as this world is, things are bound to get worse, you know."

Luke could scarcely comprehend the concept of being with Hayley forever, but he was committed to do everything in his power to insure that it would happen. For reasons he could barely comprehend, Hayley loved him, too. Whenever she left for work as a registered nurse at the hospital, they'd always say, "I love you forever" to each other. To Luke, the concept of eternity was a new one, and pretty amazing, so he latched onto it. Still, he avoided saying the phrase in public.

Luke and Hayley lived in a modest home in Helaman and attended the same ward that Hayley grew up in, and the same ward that Luke had invaded when he arrived from New York. Together they read scriptures and prayed daily. She made him want to be the best man, the best husband, he could be. He didn't want to ever hurt or disappoint her. Luke never missed a month in his hometeaching assignments and though fasting for a whole twenty-four hours was still a struggle, he did his best not to complain.

Though the Mannings were somewhat strapped for cash, Luke would bring home flowers for Hayley every week. On Saturdays, they'd take long drives up the canyon and have picnics, and explore mountain trails. He loved her so much that he didn't mind vacuuming, cleaning the bathroom, and planting tulips and daisies in the front yard.

Brother Munchak's voice rose a couple of decibels.

"It's frightening, isn't it?" he said. "In the Last Days, ancient and modern prophets say there will be earthquakes, droughts, famines, diseases, hailstorms, plagues, pestilences, and calamities. Men's hearts will fail them. Let me take a moment and ask this: Are you prepared? Do you have your year's supply of food and water, as our leaders have been asking us to do for years? Is your family ready to confront a catastrophic setback? In my business, I am fortunate enough to help others reach a state of prepared- ness and peace. If you need any help in those ways, feel free to use me as a resource. Or you can access *www.munchakmunchies.com* on the Internet to find out more about protecting your family."

Luke rolled his eyes.

"I thought church was a commercial-free zone," he said to Hayley, who let out a giggle.

"Shhhhh," she whispered. "Brother Munchak will hear you."

As happy as Luke was with Hayley, his new life wasn't all sparkling non-alcoholic cider and roses.

Much to his dismay, he had gained twelve pounds since the wedding. Talk about tribulation.

Luke had heard the horror stories before getting married about adding a spare tire to his midsection—which he was told he would keep until the Resurrection—but he never believed it would happen to him. He found himself adopting more of a sedentary lifestyle than he'd had when he was single. Hayley's patented country-fried chicken and honey-butter scones didn't help matters either.

Worse, Luke's freelance writing career had fallen on hard times. From a professional standpoint, he was beset by an overwhelming sense of discontent. He felt restless, unfulfilled, and frustrated. After several years of seeing his byline in the New York newspapers and covering exhilarating stories, Luke had to resign himself to writing for small, local papers and magazines. He wrote articles at six cents per word for the *Helaman Gazette*, punching out 2,000 words on a scrapbooking convention or an article on a new book boasting 1,001 recipes for food storage wheat.

With his newfound perspective and marital status, Luke didn't want to go back to the grind and the pressure of working at a large-circulation newspaper. So he spent a lot of time at home, sending out story ideas to editors of national magazines. But he always received rejection letters in the mail a couple of months later. The curse of Jack Kilborn, apparently, was still in full effect. Luke was convinced there was a conspiracy involved somehow. The book—which brought Luke to Helaman, Utah, and turned his life upside down—was never published, and for that, he was thankful. Kilborn, the cantankerous publisher from New York who commissioned him to write the book and sent him to Utah in the first place, warned Luke that he would be blackballed from journalism jobs. It seemed that Kilborn's prophecy was being fulfilled. Luke imagined Kilborn being fired from his job and shuffling along Broadway in a bathrobe with disheveled hair and holding out a tin cup. He enjoyed that mental image, until he realized it wasn't very Christlike.

Luke could have applied for journalism jobs around the country, but he didn't want to uproot Hayley from her family. She was, after all, Brother Grit Woodard's only daughter. If he tried taking her out of state, he knew Grit would hunt him down and gut him like a rainbow trout. What's more, he struggled to reconcile within himself his job and his religious beliefs. Could a hard-nosed journalist still be relatively conservative? His nature, his training, was to trust no one, to question everyone, especially leaders. As a member of the Church, he was taught to accept what he was told by his leaders.

During Sunday School, Luke scanned the room and he realized that every man in there but him had a stable job and made more money than he did. Then his eyes rested on Brother Helton, an attorney who had moved into the ward from California. Brother Helton wore an $800 suit that reminded Luke of the type of clothing he used to buy when he was single, living in the Big Apple, and enjoying a robust income. Luke started wondering how much money Brother Helton pulled down a year, but that only depressed him further. Here he was in his thirties and he was undergoing a process of self-discovery. He hoped he wasn't mired in a mid-life crisis already.

Hayley, who worked five days a week, was more or less the breadwinner of the family, which she didn't mind, at least until children came. Because Hayley felt she was getting up there in age—she was approaching her late twenties, which, she kept reminding Luke, was ancient by Mormon standards—she and Luke had been trying to start a family since their honeymoon. She was beginning to wonder if she could have children. She read books and consulted with a couple of specialists she knew from the hospital. They told her to be patient and if she didn't get pregnant in the next six months, they would perform some medical tests.

Secretly, Luke harbored the fear that their inability to have children was his fault. He understood the concept of baptism, and how it washed away all of his sins. He believed the Lord would forgive and forget, but he had a difficult time doing the same for himself. He was ashamed of the person he had been prior to baptism and he tried hard not to think of his past mistakes.

Luke wanted children, too, especially because he knew Hayley's fondest wish was to be a mother, and he knew she'd be a Hall-of-Fame caliber mom. If there were one gift he would love to share with her, it would parenthood. Luke secretly wanted a son, a boy he could play catch with and take to ball games.

"Brother Manning," Brother Munchak called out suddenly, his black unibrow dancing upward. "Do you have any thoughts on this subject?"

Luke thought about asking what subject he was referring to,

but instead cleared his throat to stall for time. Fortunately for him, Brother Munchak kept talking.

"I was just thinking that since you're from New York City, you probably know what the Lord is talking about here in D&C 88 where it says, 'And all things shall be in commotion.'"

Usually, Luke was never at a loss for words. He stammered for a moment when Hayley raised her hand. "Why do you think he moved to Utah?" she said, as the class laughed.

"Thanks," Luke whispered to Hayley.

"That's what wives are for," she whispered back.

"Evil, it seems, is everywhere," Brother Munchak continued. "I find it hard to watch the news anymore. I'd bet that when the Lord showed our day to ancient prophets, like Moroni, they probably saw television newscasts and a few sitcoms. Packaged in 30-minute segments on that remote-controlled box, we see how wicked this world is becoming every day. How can we have faith when there is so much negativity swirling around us?"

Brother Munchak unfurled a large map of the world and taped it over the chalkboard for everyone to see. Then he picked up a copy of that morning's newspaper.

"I'll just randomly read the headlines and we can see what's going on in the world," he said. "Adversity is around us every-where, and we're constantly being reminded of that."

Fourteen killed in terrorist attack in Israel.
Earthquake death toll soars to 136 in Mexico.
Mad cow disease discovered in Rhode Island.

"Brother Manning, I know you are a newspaper reporter by trade and I hope you don't take offense when I say this, but it seems reporters thrive on showing us all the bad things in the world. That's why I don't even bother to watch the news anymore. I actually cut off the cords on our TV just last week. The media likes to accentuate the negative. That's a big part of the problems we have."

Luke tried to be as calm as possible.

"It's true that watching the news can be discouraging," Luke said, "but it's not a reflection of the whole world. You all know as well as I do that there is a lot of good out there. News, as defined in part by journalists, is something unusual, something that doesn't happen every day. When a Boy Scout helps a little old lady across the street, that's not news. If the newscasts are filled with thirty minutes of good things, that's when I'd be worried. That would indicate that goodness is rare. It's not as rare as it is portrayed to be on TV, we all know that. Goodness is everywhere. Each of us can create goodness on our own, in our own little worlds."

"Nice comeback," Hayley whispered.

Brother Munchak titled his head heavenward, as if lost in thought. "Brother Manning," he said, "that was a very insightful comment. I hadn't thought of that before. That's what I like best about you. You always have a different way of seeing things. We really appreciate you being in our midst. You add so much to our ward."

"Thanks," Luke said. "I do what I can."

Brother Munchak then told the story about how he started his company and how he and his family had to make great sacrifices. He recalled the time when he and his wife took the kids to Deseret Industries to buy back-to-school clothing because they were so poor. Then he referred to the scripture that says "after much tribulation come the blessings."

"So," Brother Munchak asked the class, "how do we endure while we're passing through tribulation?"

Hayley raised her hand. Like a confident returned missionary, she explained that while trials and tribulations aren't fun to go through, they make us stronger. "It's all part of our Heavenly Father's plan," she said. "I certainly don't pray for trials, because trials will always find us. Still, when I look back at the most difficult times of my life, I now recall them fondly because they taught me so much. We've got to keep that perspective when times are tough."

"I think you should be teaching this class," Luke whispered in her ear.

Brother Munchak told about the Prophet Joseph Smith being imprisoned at Liberty Jail in March, 1839. "While he was there, the Prophet received revelations from the Lord about tribulation that are applicable to all of us today," he said.

The class turned with him in the D&C, and then Brother Munchak asked Luke to read Section 122, verses 7 and 8:

And if thou shouldst be cast into the pit, or into the hands of mur-derers, and the sentence of death passed upon thee; if thou be cast into the deep; if the billowing surge conspire against thee; if fierce winds become thine enemy; if the heavens gather blackness, and all the elements combine to hedge up the way; and above all, if the very jaws of hell shall gape open the mouth wide after thee, know thou, my son, that all these things shall give thee experience, and shall be for thy good. The Son of Man hath descended below them all. Art thou greater than he?

Luke marked that passage of scripture with his red pencil.

2

Three doors down from where Sunday School was wrapping up, Ben Kimball was taking care of some urgent Helaman 6th Ward business. Should the Elder's Quorum or the Activities Committee be assigned to set up chairs for the upcoming ward party?

While deep in thought over this dilemma that potentially could set the congregation at odds, he was interrupted by one of the ward clerks.

"Bishop," Brother Rose said, "there are some kids skateboarding and rollerblading in the parking lot again, disrupting some Primary classes. What would you like me to do?"

That word—*bishop*. When Ben heard it, his initial instinct was to look around for Bishop Law. He still wasn't used to responding to that title.

"Go find Brother Gruber," Ben said. "Just send him out there and he'll scare them away just by looking at them."

Brother Gruber had been inactive for years before returning to the fold and eventually becoming one of Ben's counselors. It had come as a shock of sorts when Ben was called to be the bishop a few months earlier. Then when he named Brother Gruber— a man who only a couple of years earlier was known around the ward for his prodigious ability to swill beer and curse, often simultaneously—as a counselor, well, some folks had their testimonies shaken a bit. Ben was a little surprised, too, when he felt inspired to select Brother Gruber, but he wasn't about to argue with the Lord. He remembered that Saul was quite the rabble-rouser until he experienced a change of heart and became Paul. In the previous year or so, Brother Gruber had become humble, kind, and service-oriented. In other words, Brother Gruber, like Luke, had done a Starsky-and-Hutch-like180-degree turn.

When Ben showed up for an unexpected interview with the stake president a couple of months earlier, he had no idea that it would change his life. The stake president extended the calling matter-of-factly, right after greeting him and welcoming him into his office. There was no protracted preamble or small talk. He got right to the point.

"Brother Kimball, the Lord has called you to be the next bishop of the Helaman 6th Ward. Will you accept this calling?"

Ben just sat there in a state of stupor for about one minute. Every mistake, sin, and error in judgment flooded his mind in an instant, including the time he cheated on a biology exam in junior high and the time he swiped a pack of banana-flavored Bubbalicious from a gas station when he was six.

"I know the Lord is never wrong," Ben said, chuckling nervously, "but do you think there's a possibility that He may have made a mistake on this one?"

"What makes you ask that?" asked the stake president. "Is there something amiss in your life we need to talk about?"

Ben didn't know how to answer that. If he said no, then it would look like he was boasting about his righteousness. If he said yes, then the stake president would begin to ask more uncomfortable, probing questions.

"I, um, I guess I just never thought I would be called to this kind of high position. I mean, a bishop! I've never even been an Elder's Quorum president or in any sort of presidency. I figured I was a Primary teacher for life. Which, may I add, I have no problem with. Besides, I'm certainly not perfect, I mean, I have a lot of things I need to work on. I'm not sure I'm old enough to handle this type of responsibility . . ."

"In the Lord's eyes, you must be ready," the stake president said. "He will make you equal to the task. I want you to go home and ask the Lord Himself if you're supposed to lead the ward."

Ben did just that, and the answer was yes.

It wasn't as if he didn't have enough responsibilities already—what with four children and being the manager of Kimball's Market. He still felt vulnerable at times because there were days when he'd be driving home and hear a certain song or see a group of young girls playing together and that would make him think of Brooklyn and the car accident that took her young life. Then he'd break down and sob uncontrollably. He knew she was in a far better place, but he constantly wondered where she was, who she was spending time with, what she was doing. Every time he laughed or was having fun with his family, his heart still ached, wishing Brooklyn were there to enjoy it with them.

Wasn't a bishop supposed to be in supreme control of his emotions? Ben thought. His predecessor, the legendary Bishop Law, always seemed to be. Ben was in his mid-thirties. How could he do the job that the fifty-something Bishop Law did so remarkably? It seemed impossible.

Among the tasks that scared Ben most about being a bishop were conducting temple recommend interviews, being responsible for the tithing and fast offerings, and basically being accountable for everyone within the Helaman 6th Ward boundaries. It seemed overwhelming. He never felt like that before he was the bishop.

Sometimes, Ben got the feeling people were avoiding him, as if they knew he wanted to talk to them about their church calling or ask them to speak in sacrament meeting. Some people, he thought, would practically run the other way when they saw him.

Ben knew he wasn't the only one making a big transition. Stacie's job of taking care of the kids by herself during sacrament meeting was an onerous task, too. Every Sunday, while he was off to his early-morning meetings, she had to get all four kids ready by herself. They'd usually trickle in just before the sacrament. While he was up on the stand, he would gaze down on them. It made him miss Brooklyn even more.

Being a rookie bishop meant making a lot of decisions and a few mistakes. For example, that very morning as he conducted sacrament meeting, he called for the opening prayer before the opening hymn. He didn't realize the gaffe until the congregation was about halfway through the third verse of "In Our Lovely Deseret."

If that weren't enough, Ben feared what others in the ward would think of him—Sister Fidrych, in particular. She had started a rumor in Relief Society about an upcoming change in the bishopric and she not-so-subtly implied that her husband would be replacing Bishop Law. It was almost as if she was stumping on behalf of her husband. Someone must have forgotten to tell her that when it came to matters of Church leadership, there was no such thing as a general election.

"Did you know he has not missed a single month of home-teaching in over six years?" she had told several Relief Society sisters. "The one time he did miss was when he had bronchial pneumonia. But he still called his families on the phone and had me drop off brownies for them. He is so spiritual. Did you know his patriarchal blessing says he will one day be a Judge in Israel?"

The day Ben was sustained as the bishop, Sister Fidrych began coughing uncontrollably, which forced her to walk out of the meeting. There were reports of her sitting in the foyer, madly fanning herself with a program. Word had it that she was sure there had been an oversight of some sort.

"But he's so young," she'd tell anybody who would listen. "Ben's never even been in a presidency!"

Mostly, though, ward members were very supportive and happy that Ben was their new ecclesiastical leader. Nonetheless, Ben battled feelings of inadequacy. Bishop Law, after all, left some size XXXL shoes to fill. He wasn't just a bishop, he was an icon of sorts in the neighborhood. Ben often went to Bishop Law for advice, but he wasn't much help. Bishop Law would just nod knowingly and smile. Ben hated it when he did that.

So Ben would press him and Bishop Law would respond, "Ben, if I tell you how to handle this, how are you going to learn? I'm retired from being a bishop. Now I get to sit back and watch someone else squirm. You were called to this position at this time for a reason. Rely on the Lord, Ben. He'll help you. Take it from the voice of experience. He makes up for your shortcomings somehow. Remember, this is His work, not yours."

Ben continued a tradition started by Bishop Law, acknowledging the birthday of each child in the ward with a personal visit. He put his own twist on the tradition by giving each one a coupon for a free twisty ice cream cone at his store. Still, he desperately wanted to put his own imprint on the ward, but how?

Ben noticed there seemed to be a few cliques that had emerged in the congregation. Some of the wealthier people in the ward invited those in their neighborhoods to bunco parties and get-togethers, leaving out the poorer people. Ben prayed that he would find a way to unify the ward.

When, as a brand-new bishop, Ben met with the other bishops in the stake, he was eager to learn all he could. He was also eager to make an impression, to move out from the huge shadow left by Bishop Law. The stake president encouraged every bishop to organize a ward humanitarian effort during the holiday season and Ben's ears perked up. He figured a service project could really unite the ward, bring blessings into the members' lives, and strengthen their confidence in their new bishop. At least, that's what he hoped.

And he knew just the person to help him accomplish this feat.

3

Monday afternoon, during a lunch break, Ben left his store and dropped in on Luke at home.

"Hi, Bishop," Luke said when he saw Ben standing on the porch.

"You don't need to call me Bishop. At least not when we're out of a church setting," Ben said.

"So, you're not here in the capacity of a bishop?" Luke asked.

"Well, yes and no."

"How can you expect me to carry on a conversation with you if I don't even know what to call you?"

"Can I come in?" Ben said with a laugh.

"Yeah. It sounds like we're in for a long conversation," Luke said as they sat down on the couch.

"Hayley's at work, I presume?" Ben asked.

"Yeah, 'til seven."

"What are you watching?"

"The Scrabble All-Star Championships," Luke said sheepishly. "It's actually quite riveting."

Luke picked up the remote control and clicked off the TV.

"Are you here to give me a new calling?" Luke asked. "I've been the building facilities coordinator for almost a year now. By the way, is that a made up calling? It sounds made up."

"No, it's not made up," Ben said. "But if you complain about it, I'll make you the Scoutmaster."

"Oh, believe me, I'm not complaining," Luke said. "The real perk of this calling is that I can go to the church whenever I want to shoot hoops in the cultural hall."

"Scheduling the cultural hall, setting up chairs, putting hymnbooks on the benches, and vacuuming up Cheerios on the chapel floor is a valuable, though thankless, service to the ward. And last week when the microphone went out during Sister Wilmsmeyer's testimony, I was proud of the way you rushed out of the meeting and found one that worked. Anyway, I'm not here about your calling."

"Then what is it?"

"I may have a great story for you to write about."

"Ben, as much as I enjoyed it, you know I can't do another five-part series for the *Helaman Gazette* on how to pick a ripe cantaloupe at Kimball's Market."

"No, it's nothing like that," Ben replied. "The stake is making a big push for humanitarian efforts and we're going to be involved in that this fall. A lot of the wards are putting together hygiene kits and food supplies for people in third-world countries. The only problem is when you do that, you never get to see the difference you've made in the lives of those people."

"That is nice and all," Luke said, "but what does this have to do with me and my writing career?"

"I was thinking that maybe we could send one of our ward members to a third-world country to witness and chronicle what happens with all of the humanitarian items that we gather. I'll give you one guess who's name came to mind."

"Sister Fidrych?"

Ben ignored Luke's sarcasm, as usual. "I know you're looking for stories to write and this would be a great one. I was thinking maybe you could go somewhere and personally deliver all the stuff we collect. It sounds a little crazy, but you could write about your experiences. You could personalize the giving of gifts to complete strangers somewhere in the world. I'm sure our ward members would be thrilled to read it and I bet there are newspapers and magazines that would publish your story."

Luke got off the couch and started pacing across the floor. "You know, that's not a bad idea," he said. He then ambled over to the living room window. "It could be a great feel-good holiday story. Maybe I could do a story for *Time* or *Newsweek*."

"And there's always the *Ensign*," Ben said as Luke's smile vanished. "The only trouble is, I don't know how you'd get to one of those countries, let alone with all of our donations. I wonder if there is some humanitarian group that you could go with?"

"I don't know," Luke said, "but I'm going to find out right now." For the first time in years, he was genuinely excited about a work-related task. "I wonder what Hayley will think about this?" Luke said.

"May I give you a little piece of advice from a man who's been married awhile?" Ben asked.

"I'm all ears."

"Break it to her very gently. She probably won't be as thrilled about this idea as we are."

As soon as Ben left, Luke logged onto the Internet and began a search for humanitarian groups. He spent the balance of the day researching and making phone calls. Then, finally, he found an international relief organization called Samaritans Around the World, run by a church based in Dallas. Luke learned that the group traveled to the African nation of Sudan a few times a year.

Luke called the general number and worked his way up until he contacted the president of the non-profit organization, Reverend Bobby Thurgood.

After explaining that he would like to collect donations and take them on their next trip to Sudan in November, Reverend Thurgood interrupted Luke.

"I applaud you for your desire to help. Are you a Christian, young man?" Thurgood asked.

"Absolutely," Luke replied. "I was born again a couple of years ago. Believe me, my life hasn't been the same since."

"Glad to hear that," Thurgood said. "We want to make sure that if we have you with us that we receive good publicity."

"I'm sure you'll receive plenty of good publicity," Luke said.

"It's highly unusual for us to allow a reporter to go along with us," Reverend Thurgood said. "There are precious few seats on our planes that go to Sudan. Will you be willing to help out?"

"Absolutely," Luke said. "What would you want me to do?"

"You may be asked to help unload supplies or assist the doctors with patients, things like that."

"Okay."

"And I should let you know that Sudan is no picnic. It's basically a war zone and an international disaster area. In other words, I can't guarantee your safety. But if you stick with the members of our organization, you should be in good hands, Lord willing. Any questions?"

"Just one," Luke said. "When do we leave?"

Then the two talked about travel plans and what Luke would have to do in the ensuing months to prepare for the trip. The group wanted him to sign a waiver and then make a monetary donation to Samaritans Around the World to help defray some of the travel costs. Luke told Reverend Thurgood he would be in touch again soon.

When he got off the phone, story ideas were leaking out of his ears. Luke excitedly pulled out a globe that he and Hayley had received as a wedding present and located Sudan. Then he called Ben and told him the news.

"You know, I could probably find a bunch of interesting stories over there," Luke said excitedly. "From what I know about Sudan, there are always civil wars, famine, military coups—never a dull moment. If I stayed about a week, I could have enough material to write several articles of national interest."

"Have you told Hayley about this yet?" Ben asked.

"No."

"Maybe you should do that before you go any further."

Luke racked his brain, trying to figure out how he could broach the subject with Hayley. Then he formulated a plan. He pored over Hayley's cookbooks and whipped up a chicken-and-broccoli casserole. Besides burning a hole in the table cloth, it went off without a hitch. Just before Hayley returned home from her long shift at the hospital, he dimmed the lights and lit a few candles.

4

The idea of going to Africa grew on Luke and not just because it was an opportunity to write interesting stories. He always liked hearing missionary stories Ben and Hayley told him. It made him wish he could have served a mission. He and Hayley discussed going on a mission when they got older, but he knew it wouldn't be the same. By going to Sudan, he thought, it could be his version of a mission on a much smaller, and shorter scale. A two-week mission to a far-flung locale, a place where missionaries aren't allowed to go—there was something mysterious and adventurous about it all.

Before Hayley came home from work, Luke showered and shaved for the second time that day. When he lived in New York, he liked having the *Miami Vice* five o'clock shadow look, but that didn't seem to go over well in Helaman. Besides, for Hayley, he tried to maintain BYU-approved hair and grooming standards. As a member of the Church, he shaved everyday, including Saturdays—in large part because he knew Hayley preferred kissing him when he was clean-shaven.

Luke couldn't quite understand the Church's aversion to facial hair, seeing as how Jesus and Brigham Young wore beards during their ministries. He never brought it up, but he did notice that very few people had facial hair—with a notable exception being Sister Luzinski. Then again, she had a medical condition.

When Hayley walked through the door that night, she saw Luke sitting on the couch wearing a suit and a smile.

"I'm sorry," she said. "I thought for a moment this was my house."

"You're in the right place," Luke said.

"Oh no," Hayley said, "is it ward temple night?"

"No," Luke said as he gave her a hug.

"What is all this?" she asked.

"Dinner. This time, it didn't come from A Wok-To-Remember."

"It's not our anniversary, you know."

"Yeah, I know."

"You haven't made dinner like this for me since we were dating."

"You should be grateful for that," Luke replied.

"What's the occasion?"

"No occasion. I just thought you had a long day and instead of doing the usual and ordering Chinese, I wanted to do something a little different."

"A little?" Hayley said. She slipped off her shoes and plopped down on the couch. He took a seat next to her and she lay her head on his shoulder.

"How was your day?" Luke asked.

"I don't even want to think about it. I might have set the world record for the most bedpans cleaned in a twelve-hour stretch."

"On that note, how about we eat?"

"I'm starved," she said.

Luke stood up, helped her off the couch and into her chair.

"Are you sure you're feeling okay?" she asked.

"Yeah," he said. "My best day yet."

Luke offered the blessing on the food and they started to eat.

"This is very good," Hayley said, chewing on a piece of chicken. "You sure Stacie didn't make this?"

"I tried to get her help," Luke admitted, "but she was busy."

"She's got four kids and is the bishop's wife," Hayley said. "Go figure."

During dessert—ice cream sandwiches—Luke finally got

down to business. He told her all about this opportunity to go on a humanitarian trip to Sudan.

"I knew you had some ulterior motive," Hayley said. "Isn't that a dangerous place?"

"Is it?" Luke said, feigning ignorance. "Well, it's probably not a place Martha Stewart goes on vacation."

"Luke, are you seriously considering this? Is it worth it to go that far to write some stories?"

"It's only for a couple of weeks. This is what I love to do. You know—the challenge, the mystery, the danger of it all."

Looking into her eyes, he knew he had gone too far.

Just before Hayley burst into tears, she stood up and marched to the bathroom.

"That could have gone better," Luke said to himself as he followed her.

From outside the bathroom door, he listened to her muffled sobs.

"We've been married for about a year," she said, "and you want to go traipsing off to Africa?"

"This isn't about marriage, Hayley," Luke said. "This is about my profession."

As soon as those words left his lips, he realized he was in even deeper trouble.

Like any couple, they experienced some spats during their marriage. This was the biggest one to date.

That night as he lay awake, and alone, on the couch, the one with the bad spring stabbing him in the back, he thought about his marriage and how it was far more important than everything else in his life. He didn't want to jeopardize it in any way.

Luke turned on the lamp next to the couch, and then picked up a photo album that Hayley had made of their dating years. He remembered the day, ten months after his baptism, when he and Hayley were strolling hand in hand around Temple Square. Luke unabashedly knelt down before her in front of the Visitors Center and asked her to marry him. Once she overcame the initial shock, she smiled, bent down to hug him, and said yes.

While they were dating, Hayley would complain to Luke because she thought he drove his red corvette too fast. She warned him repeatedly about that dangerous habit. Well, on their wedding day, Luke drove to the temple alone while Hayley went with her parents. They had been asked to show up at the temple a good two hours early. Luke arrived in the waiting area of the Salt Lake Temple and waited for his bride-to-be. And waited. And waited. Luke nervously paced the floor. The octogenarian temple workers in the foyer couldn't resist teasing him.

"Don't worry, a lot of young fellows get left at the altar," they said with a gleam in their eyes.

Luke didn't see the humor in it.

Maybe, he thought, Hayley's father had talked sense into her. Maybe she realized that she could do much better than some wild-eyed, fast-talking, Corvette-driving convert from New York City with a questionable past.

Finally, after Luke had spent an hour wearing out the carpet in the waiting area, Hayley arrived, a bundle of nerves. Luke could tell she had been crying. Fearing the worst, he approached her cautiously.

"We were running late and I decided I should drive," she said, wiping a mascara streak from her cheek. "I got a speeding ticket. Can you believe that? I've never had a ticket in my life. The highway patrol guy didn't give me a warning. He gave me a ticket—on my wedding day!"

Luke laughed in sheer relief. "I've been telling you that you really need to slow down."

They didn't have a lot of money, so the honeymoon was simple. They drove their green minivan—Hayley had convinced him to sell the Corvette for a more family-friendly mode of transportation—to Northern California. While passing through Nevada on a Sunday afternoon, they couldn't find a church to attend, so Hayley compensated by turning off the football game on the radio and playing Mormon Tabernacle Choir CDs. After a while, she began singing and she made Luke sing too. He lightheartedly protested, but for her, he'd do anything.

Throughout the day, they sang all the verses of all of the Church hymn classics. By honeymoon's end, Luke had memorized all the verses of "High On A Mountain Top," "The Spirit of God" and "Give Said The Little Stream."

"One of the best things about this Church is the hymns," Hayley told Luke during a break between songs. "When I was on my mission, whenever times got rough, we'd sing hymns and it was amazing how they would lift our spirits."

"One day of marriage and times are rough already?" Luke said rakishly.

Hayley laughed and caressed the back of his head. "You'll thank me for teaching you these hymns someday," she said.

"I'm sure I will," Luke replied. "I just wish Jimmy Buffett would write some hymns. It might liven things up at church a little."

"Yeah, well, William W. Phelps is the Mormon version of Jimmy Buffet," Hayley replied. "Nothing compares to the songs he's written."

"Like what?"

"Like 'Praise To The Man,' 'Now Let Us Rejoice,' and 'The Spirit of God.'"

Then she began singing "The Spirit of God." By the second verse, she made Luke sing, too. Midway through, she stopped. "You have to do it *exultantly*," she said.

"*Exultantly?*"

"Yeah. You know, like you know that in the end, everything will be fine."

"Kind of that 'all is well' feeling, you mean?"

"Exactly."

Once the newlyweds settled down, Hayley set up some house rules—one of them was no television on Sundays. But she usually let him watch the ten o'clock news to catch the sports scores and highlights. It was their version of the Great Compromise.

On Luke's birthday, Hayley gave him a monogrammed journal. Every week Hayley wrote faithfully in her journal but Luke struggled to do the same.

"You're a writer. Why don't you write in your journal?"

"Nothing exciting ever happens to me anymore," Luke replied.

Noticing the hurt look on her face, Luke realized he had committed a verbal faux pas of the worst kind. "What I mean is, my life's different than it used to be, and that's a good thing," he said. "But I am excited every morning to wake up because I know I get a chance to live another day with you."

"Nice recovery," Hayley said.

Hayley served as the ward organist. One of the downsides for Luke was having to sit on the front row every week and knowing he had to sing every word of every song. Hayley could tell if he was just mouthing the words and if he was, he'd hear about it.

Luke accompanied her to the church every Saturday afternoon so she could practice the hymns for sacrament meeting the next day.

"Luke, go stand up front and pretend you're leading the music," she'd say. Hayley had taught him all about measures, time signatures, and downbeats. He'd fake his way through it, waving his arms in a flurry like the director of the New York Philharmonic, or directing New York traffic during rush hour. Not only that, she'd make him sing all the words aloud as she played. One time, a group of young priests in the ward showed up to play basketball and opened the chapel doors.

"Oh, it's you, Brother Manning," one of the boys called out. "I thought someone was torturing a pig in here or something."

Hayley joined the ward choir, which meant Luke joined, too. She dragged him to ward choir practice every Sunday afternoon.

More than anything, Luke wanted to make Hayley as happy as she had made him. He wanted to give her a big house, a big yard, and lots of kids—the Mormon-American dream. The house they were living in was aging, the bathroom sink had a leak, and the ceiling paint had begun to crack. Hayley deserved much better, Luke thought.

Lying on the couch, Luke could feel his neck tightening up. He didn't like being apart from Hayley, even for one night. So he decided to cancel the trip to Sudan. He told Hayley the next morning.

"I don't understand why you want to go so far away," she said.

"I guess part of it is because I keep hearing all these stories you and Ben tell about your missions and how they helped you in your lives. I never got the chance to go on a mission. I was thinking this could be mine. A mini-mission, where I can selflessly help others. I don't know, it sounded like a good idea at the time. But you're right. I was wrong. You come first in my life and I wasn't thinking of you, of us."

"Thank you for understanding," Hayley said as she hugged him.

Though he was disappointed, Luke spent the next few days spontaneously cleaning the bathroom and the garage. It was his way of apologizing. Then, one night while he was helping Hayley with the dishes, and as the Mormon Tabernacle Choir CD played in the background, she took his hand and turned toward him.

"I've been doing a lot of thinking about that trip to Sudan," she said. "I really think you should go."

"What, are you mad at me again?"

"No," she said. "I love you and that's why I want you to go. You remind me of a dog my dad once had."

"I'm flattered," Luke said.

"Let me explain," Hayley said with a grin. "He had this dog, Butch. I think he was a cross between a springer spaniel and a black lab. Anyway, Dad wanted to train Butch to be a nice little house dog for me to play with so he always kept him fenced in. Well, Butch kept getting out under the fence. No matter how many boulders Dad would put under the fence to keep him in, Butch always found a way out. Once, he was missing for days. I thought he was lost or dead or had been picked up by the pound. Then one morning he showed up out of the blue with porcupine quills all over his nose. So Dad chained him up and all Butch did all day and all night was bark and bark and bark and make this whining noise. Finally, Dad decided that Butch wasn't meant to live that way. He realized he was trying to force him to be something he wasn't. Butch wasn't happy. Luke, I want you to be happy."

"Hayley, I am happy," Luke said.

28

"I know. But there's something that makes you who you are. You like adventure. You like uncovering stories and telling them to people. That's one of the things I love about you. I was pretty selfish for telling you not to go to Africa. Besides, this could be a big benefit to the ward, the people of Sudan, not to mention to you. What you said about a chance to serve a mission really struck me. Call those people in Dallas. Tell them that you're going after all."

"Are you sure about this?"

"Not completely," she said, "but while I was working today, I thought of those poor kids in Africa who live in such terrible conditions. Then I thought of what the Lord said. You know, the part about 'inasmuch as ye have done it unto one of the least of these my brethren, ye have done it unto me.' I'm committed to helping others everyday at work. Why should I deny you that opportunity? I've tried to look at this from your perspective. I know journalism is a big part of who you are, just as nursing is a big part of who I am. By denying you this trip, I would be denying you happiness. As much as I don't like the thought of you being away from me, I know the Lord will watch over you."

Tears welled up in her eyes. "You should go."

Luke had never imagined he could love Hayley more than he already did.

"Thanks," he said. "I won't get a chance to teach the gospel there since proselytizing is not allowed, plus there's that little matter of not being able to speak Sudanese or whatever they speak over there. But it's probably as close to going on a mission as I'm going to get."

"Just promise me one thing," she said as she turned on the dishwasher.

"Anything," Luke said, drying his hands on the dish towel that hung on the refrigerator.

"Promise me that you'll be safe."

"I promise," Luke said, pulling her close. "I love you forever."

"I love you forever."

5

A Dallas doctor, Owen Allman, who was part of Samaritans Around the World, called Luke one afternoon. He had been in Sudan several times on humanitarian trips and told Luke he would be going with him in November.

"Ever run into trouble over there?" Luke asked.

"Never," he said. "Don't get me wrong, it's a dangerous place, but the Lord protects us."

"What's it like over there?"

"It's heartbreaking. You'll love the people. There sure is a lot of sadness in their lives. It's nice to know there are reporters out there who are Christian. You don't find many of those. What congregation do you belong to?"

"It's a little church out in Utah. The Mormon Church. Maybe you've heard of it."

There was a long pause on the other end of the phone. "You never said you were a Mormon," Dr. Allman finally said.

"Reverend Thurgood asked me if I were a Christian," Luke said. "I am."

"That's debatable," muttered Dr. Allman under his breath. "In any case, we welcome everyone who would like to serve their brothers and sisters in places like Sudan. We're taking Christ's message of love and peace to people who are suffering immensely. We need people to help in our ministry. Some black Africans have been sold into slavery, hundreds of others have been slaughtered. It's just like what Hitler did to the Jews. It's a modern day Holocaust. And it's our responsibility to do something about it.

Hundreds of Sudanese children are dying every day from starvation and diseases like polio and malaria."

"What can the people in my congregation gather for the Sudanese people?" Luke asked. "What is it they need?"

"Well," Dr. Allman said, "we usually provide them food and medicine. I feel so badly for the children. They have very little. They lack simple pleasures, like toys. Maybe you could gather toys—dolls, balls, trucks. Just thinking of those poor kids breaks my heart. It brings tears to my eyes. A toy would mean the world to them, a bit of joy amid so much unhappiness."

All the arrangements were made for the 7,940-mile flight to Khartoum, the capital city of Sudan. Dr. Allman told Luke they would fly into Khartoum and stay there one night before going on to various parts of the country.

In a matter of days, Luke devoured everything he could about Sudan, which is located in northeastern Africa. Luke studied the map and noticed that Sudan looked like the keystone of the continent. The largest country in Africa in terms of size, Sudan's borders touch, going clockwise and starting in the north: Egypt, the Red Sea, Eritea, Ethiopia, Kenya, Uganda, Zaire, the Central African Republic, Chad, and Libya. The mighty Nile River cuts a swath right through the heart of the country.

The more he read and studied about the strife in Sudan, the more Luke realized how dangerous a place it was. It had been mired in a twenty-year-old civil war. While the entire country was weary of hostilities, they could not establish a peace treaty. To some, it appeared imminent. Others expressed doubt that there would ever be a lasting peace in Sudan.

According to an ancient Sudanese proverb, when Allah created Sudan, he laughed in delight. Reality was, there was little in the harsh region to even smile about.

Sudan was home to the world's longest-running war, which had left about two million dead and turned another six million into refugees.

While reading a book about the country, Luke learned the

majority of its people are Muslim and very conservative. Years earlier, strict Islamic law—known as sharia—was imposed all over the country, including the south, which escalated the civil war there. As part of sharia, alcohol is prohibited and conservative dress is the norm. Women wear long-sleeved shirts and full-length skirts or pants. Men are allowed to wear short-sleeved shirts, but cannot wear shorts in public.

Doesn't sound that much different from Utah, Luke thought.

The goal of Samaritans Around the World, Dr. Allman told him, was to help the Christians there effect a peace treaty and be free to preach the gospel throughout Sudan.

The group had built a hospital and a medical clinic there, both of which had been bombed by the Sudanese government. The government had also demolished a number of Christian churches. Millions of Sudanese people had been displaced from their homes.

Reverend Thurgood was determined to succeed in Sudan. He had visited the country many times and established a some-what good relationship with the government. He agreed to send doctors to help the hospitals in Khartoum at some point. Still, there was plenty of distrust on both sides. Reverend Thurgood's organization had several airplanes that were used to send in doctors and dentists, as well as humanitarian aid.

Dr. Allman told Luke some jaw-dropping stories about the Lord's Resistance Army, a band of nefarious men who roamed the land kidnapping children and converting them to their per-verted vision of the world. They brainwashed the children to kill their parents and become cannibals.

"The Sudanese government sponsors this satanic group," Dr. Allman said. "That's what we're dealing with here. This whole war boils down to religious freedom. They hate Christians. The only antidote I know for this level of evil is Jesus Christ. He can change their hearts. He can bring peace into their miserable lives. That's what keeps me going."

Reverend Thurgood explained that the average household in southern Sudan has about seven people and more than 90 percent of the people live in abject poverty. Illnesses run rampant there.

Luke logged onto the U.S. Department of State Web site and read the chilling warning: "The Department of State believes there is a credible threat of terrorist attacks against Americans in East Africa. Travelers to East African destinations should carefully review their plans accordingly."

Naturally, he didn't let Hayley in on little details like that. She even told him that the less she knew about things like that, the better. There was no way he was going to tell Hayley that Osama bin Laden had once lived in Sudan and run a terrorist training camp there.

The State Department cautioned travelers that extremists were active in East Africa and that Americans visiting that region should be vigilant. "Terrorist actions may include suicide operations, bombings, or kidnappings. Terrorists do not distinguish between official and civilian targets. Increased security at U.S. facilities has led terrorists to seek softer targets such as residential areas, clubs, restaurants, American commercial interests, Western-oriented shopping centers, places of worship, hotels, schools, outdoor recreation events, resorts, beaches, and planes. Americans in remote areas or border regions where military or police authority is limited or non-existent could also be targets of attacks or kidnappings."

From what Luke gathered, human rights issues weren't a big deal in Sudan.

Luke let out a long sigh.

"What's wrong, honey?" Hayley asked as she walked into his office.

"Nothing," he said, nonchalantly clicking off the State Department Web site.

"Are you learning a lot about Sudan?"

"Oh, yeah. Did you know they have beaches there?"

"Really?" Hayley said.

"Yeah. Right up against the Red Sea. You know, I've always wondered if the Red Sea is really red."

"Sounds interesting. Maybe we can go on a second honeymoon there someday."

"I'll check it all out while I'm there."

When she left for work, he kept reading. The information he was gathering frightened him and thrilled him at the same time.

Ever since he was in journalism school at Syracuse University, he had always dreamed of being a war correspondent. He longed to have lived during the 1960s, when he could have traveled to Vietnam to cover the war there. And after reading all about Sudan, he realized he was about to enter a war zone of sorts.

"Until the bloodshed is over," said a State Department warning, "only war correspondents and those assisting in humanitarian efforts should travel to Sudan."

The way Luke saw it, he was both a correspondent and a humanitarian aid worker. That justified it, he thought.

As if man-made problems weren't enough, Sudan seemed to be a magnet for natural disasters and health problems as well. Droughts plagued its deserts and disease ran rampant throughout the land.

Luke got right on the process of obtaining a passport and visa, both of which were required by the Sudanese government. The man he talked to at the embassy was very helpful. "Excuse me, sir, but are you crazy?" he asked.

"Quite possibly," Luke said. "Why do you ask?"

"Because you'd almost have to be to go to Sudan right now. Even the U.S. Embassy in Sudan is closed down due to civil war and terror warnings."

Still, Luke was sure the trip would be profitable, for various reasons.

The *Helaman Gazette* agreed to pay him 22 cents per word for his Sudan story. He was sure that while he was there, he could find other interesting stories that he could sell to big newspapers and national magazines. Then he got the idea of taking a video camera, too, thinking that he could produce a low-budget documentary on his trip. If nothing else, he was sure he could sell it to PBS or something.

One way or another, Luke was going to make this journey to Sudan into the turning point in his journalistic career.

Luke was going on a mission. A humanitarian mission. It was just two weeks, not two years, but he hoped that during that fortnight abroad he would experience a different culture and find new material to write about.

6

Ben made the big announcement about the upcoming ward humanitarian project in sacrament meeting the next week and the congregation became more excited than he had expected. He told the ward members that they needed to gather toys and other items and that Luke needed a couple thousand dollars for transportation, food, and lodging in Sudan. To his surprise, by the next Sunday, Luke collected enough money to cover all of his expenses. He was floored by the ward members' generosity.

For a couple of months, Ben and his counselors marshaled the ward forces for this humanitarian project to top all humanitarian projects.

Ben had heard that the Helaman 2nd Ward had made 400 quilts to be shipped to Afghanistan.

Ben knew his ward could do even better. Nobody from the 2nd ward had the guts to make the trip to Afghanistan and personally deliver those blankets. *Cowards*, he thought in jest. In his case, one of his ward members would personally deliver their goods. The stake president would be *so* impressed.

Some ward members purchased toys at a dollar store in Helaman, while others packed up old toys that weren't being used anymore. Brother Gruber actually made a few toys in the woodshop in his garage. On one Saturday, the Boy Scouts, as part of an Eagle project, fixed up, painted, and repaired the older toys. The Munchaks donated a case of their food products. Then all of the donations were covered in bright, colorful Christmas wrapping paper.

For Ben, the toughest part came when he went into Brooklyn's room in search of toys to give away. Her room had remained basically untouched from the time she had died, nearly three years earlier. It had become a shrine of sorts, a holy place where, from time to time, he'd pray. He felt close to his daughter there. Of course, he could never enter the room without the plumbing in his eyes backing up. As part of the humanitarian project, he and Stacie picked out a few dolls and other toys to give away. They knew that if Brooklyn were alive, that's the way she would have wanted it.

Luke had mentioned to Ben that he wanted to teach some Sudanese kids baseball. He bought a dozen baseballs, a few gloves, and bats. Ben noticed a baseball glove, one Luke had given Brooklyn for Christmas not long before she died. "How would you feel about us donating that glove you gave to Brooklyn to the humanitarian project?" Ben asked Luke.

"I think Brooklyn would like that," he answered without hesitating.

There was an outpouring of support from the ward and people told Luke how excited they were for him and how they couldn't wait to read his report.

Not everybody was thrilled about the project. Sister Fidrych, for instance, wondered aloud about the wisdom of sending so much to people so far away when there were children in the United States who would be going without during the holidays.

When Stacie heard that kind of talk, she wanted to stick up for her husband. She wanted to say that every child is a child of God, no matter where they live, and that there were different levels of poverty and that any child in Sudan would trade places with any child in the United States in a heartbeat. She wanted to tell Sister Fidrych to read the scripture about the Good Samaritan and remind her that the parable was the result of a lawyer asking Jesus, "Who is my neighbor?"

Instead, she kept quiet. As the bishop's wife, she had to be careful of what she said.

7

In preparation for his trip to Sudan, Luke packed a very discreet wardrobe consisting mostly of faded Levis and plain-colored, long-sleeved shirts. One thing he wanted to be in Sudan was inconspicuous, as Dr. Allman advised him.

That was fine with Luke. No white shirts and ties. That was his kind of mission.

"And don't forget a couple pairs of sandals," Dr. Allman added.

A week before his departure, ward members loaded boxes and crates of donations onto a truck that would go on to Dallas to be inspected in a processing center before being placed on the plane to Sudan.

"Brethren," Luke announced to the crowd, "thanks so much for all of your help. When we're done, come on over to the house. Hayley's been busy this morning making scones for everyone."

While loading the boxes, Luke's father-in-law, Brother Woodard, ambled over toward Luke.

Of course, Luke and Grit had a long and rocky history. Luke had met Grit long before he knew Hayley even existed. Their relationship had gotten off to a less-than-auspicious start, thanks to a ward basketball game gone awry. Grit's tooth still gave him occasional problems because of the incident.

A long time later, before Luke proposed to Hayley, he requested to talk to Grit one evening, to ask for his blessing.

"May I have a word with you, alone?" he'd asked as they sat together in the Woodards' living room after Hayley had gone

38

upstairs to do a perm on her mom's hair.

Grit didn't answer for a minute or two. He just stared at the ground. He knew what was coming.

"Okay," he finally said. "Come with me."

Grit led Luke out behind the house, into the barn. It occurred to Luke that the old man could get rid of him right then and there and he'd never be heard from again. Then again, he'd prefer a slow, painful death to Grit refusing to allow his daughter to marry him. Luke's heart was thumping wildly.

"What do you want to talk to me about?" Grit asked, leaning against a pitchfork.

Luke had rehearsed all week in preparation for this discussion, but suddenly he was drawing a blank. Then his hay fever kicked in. He sneezed a couple of times.

"Bless you," Grit said.

"Thanks," Luke said, pulling out a handkerchief. "Well, as you know, Hayley and I have been seeing each other for a while and, um, I really care for her."

Care for her? Luke thought. *Man, do I sound stupid or what?*

"I love Hayley with all of my heart," he re-stated. "I'm going to ask her to marry me. I hope you're all right with that."

Grit lifted the pitchfork off the ground.

I'm a dead man, Luke thought.

Grit didn't say a word for a full minute, filling the air with excruciating silence.

"I knew this day would probably come, the day when my little girl would be leaving me," Grit finally said. "I have to say, it's not anything like I imagined it."

Not exactly a ringing endorsement, Luke thought.

"She's my only daughter and I just want what's best for her. For some reason, she really seems to like you. I hope you can make her happy."

"I'll do everything in my power to make her happy," Luke said.

"Can I ask you one question?" Grit asked.

"Sure."

"How do you feel about children?"

Luke almost fell over into a pile of manure. "I, um, I like kids. Why?"

"Adam and Eve were given a commandment by the Lord to multiply and replenish the Earth," Grit said, "and that commandment hasn't been repealed. My daughter wants to be a mother more than anything else in this world."

"I know," Luke said. "Hayley and I have already talked about it. We want to have a whole slew of kids."

Grit nodded, but his facial expression never changed. He was resigned to the fact that Luke Manning was about to become his son-in-law. "I hope you make my daughter happy and get her to the celestial kingdom," he said, fingering the pitchfork.

No, Grit wasn't exactly thrilled about Luke becoming part of the family, but, over time, he learned to tolerate him. Though Luke had joined the Church, he was still a little too liberal for Grit's tastes. They had a classic Archie Bunker-Meathead relationship.

One Easter, the two argued about politics over roast beef and mashed potatoes. The only thing that stopped the altercation was Hayley breaking down in tears, just like Gloria in an "All In The Family" episode.

When Luke wasn't around, Grit would talk to Hayley about him.

"I'm really concerned about Luke," Grit said.

"Why, Dad?"

"I think he's a . . . *democrat*," he said softly.

Then he would ask why Luke wasn't gainfully employed. He did not like the idea of his daughter supporting their family. That just wasn't his way.

"He's between jobs," she'd say. "He'll find his niche soon."

"What happens when you start having children?"

"Dad, I appreciate your concern," she'd reply, "but you just need to trust me."

While loading toys and items on the truck, Luke was sure that Grit thought this whole idea of gallivanting around a third-world country and leaving Hayley home alone was irresponsible. He braced for a lecture.

"You return home safely, for my daughter's sake," Grit said as he approached Luke.

"I plan to, sir," Luke replied, wondering if Grit was secretly hoping this was the last time he'd have to see him. They awkwardly shook hands.

8

On the morning of his departure, the alarm sounded at five o'clock. Luke got out of bed as quietly as possible so he wouldn't wake Hayley. She had gotten home only a couple of hours earlier after a late-night shift at the hospital. He showered, dressed, and ate half a bowl of Wheaties. Luke had a bit of an unsettled stomach— whether it was caused by fear or anticipation, he wasn't sure. He was to fly from Salt Lake City to Dallas, where he would board a Samaritans Around the World-owned plane to Sudan.

He knew Hayley was exhausted, yet he longed to talk to her one last time before leaving. They had spent an entire day together earlier in the week—bowling, going out for Mexican food, watching a movie. It was the perfect day, Luke thought, a day he wished could have lasted forever.

He peeked out through the living room blinds to watch for Ben, who would be picking him up and taking him to the airport. While Luke was looking out the window, two arms embraced him from behind. He turned around and looked into Hayley's eyes.

"I'm going to miss you," Luke said. He stroked her hair and brushed her cheek with his hand.

"Me too," she whispered.

"It's just fourteen days," Luke added. "I'll be home before you know it. I'll be home in time for Thanksgiving. Save me some dark meat and stuffing, okay? Don't worry about saving me Cranberry sauce and candied yams. Just don't tell your mom. It would break her heart."

"I wish I could go with you to the airport," Hayley said.

"It's okay. You've been to the airport before. Nothing to see there, just a lot of long lines. Besides, with all of these new security measures, you can't even go to the gate. You need to get your sleep. I'll call you when I get to Dallas. And I'll e-mail or call as often as I can."

Then they saw the headlights of Ben's minivan in the driveway. Luke picked up his two bags in one arm and hugged Hayley with the other. Then he kissed her.

"I love you forever," he said.

"I love you forever."

Luke walked out the door and Hayley dead-bolted it behind him. She returned to the window and watched the minivan disappear down the street in the pre-dawn darkness.

"Be careful, Luke," she said aloud, as if he could still hear her. She wanted to go back to bed and sleep, but she couldn't. She knelt by her bed and offered a prayer, asking the Lord to watch over and protect Luke from harm.

Despite the early hour, Ben was unusually perky and chatty. Stacie had packed treats for the trip to the airport.

"Wish I were going with you," Ben said while munching on a powdered donut. "I kind of envy you."

"I'm sure Dr. Allman's got room for one more on the plane," Luke said.

Ben shook his head. "I can't leave the store behind. I'm sure the ward can survive without me, but the store is another matter. By the way, I almost forgot. I've got you scheduled to speak in sacrament meeting the Sunday after you get home."

"Great," Luke said. "One more thing to worry about."

"Are you ready to rough it for a while?" Ben asked.

"Sure. I can handle it."

"You hated camping in a tent for one night when you came on the Fathers and Sons outing. Remember?"

"I'll be fine," Luke said. "It's only two weeks."

Ben began to chuckle to himself.

"What's so funny?" Luke asked.

"I was just thinking about the time we picked up Phil

Santangelo on the side of the freeway and I made you take him in. Now look at you. You're volunteering for a humanitarian project in Africa. You've come a long way."

"Yeah, I'm going a long way, too."

When they arrived at the airport, Ben accompanied Luke to the security check area. Ben gave him one of those quick guy hugs. "Come back safe," he said.

"Why is everyone telling me that?" Luke asked.

Just his luck, Luke was "randomly selected" for a security check and was forced to practically disrobe in the airport. He had to untuck his shirt and remove his shoes, and his belt.

After finding his seat, Luke looked out of the window as the plane rose above the Wasatch Mountains. He was barely leaving Utah airspace and a part of him already couldn't wait to get back home.

When he arrived in Dallas, Luke met Dr. Allman. He was plump and balding, with a bit of white hair over his ears. Dr. Allman introduced him to a dentist, Dr. Barry Franks, who was also making the trip. Luke also met the two pilots and ten other volunteers. Most of them had been to Sudan a couple of times before and they would be staying there for up to a year.

After spending thirty minutes on the tarmac, the Samaritans Around the World jet cruised down the runway, then roared up into the graying skies. Luke opened his bag for a snack and stumbled across an envelope instead. *Hayley must have put it there when she got home from the hospital,* he thought.

Luke tore open the envelope and eagerly read the handwritten words on a piece of parchment.

Luke,

I'm sure right now I am missing you, but I'm happy that you're doing something you enjoy. I hope this is the start of something big for your writing career. I admire your desire to serve the downtrodden people in Sudan. Still, I can't wait until you get home. Hopefully, soon, you will find a job that you love and we'll have children. I can't wait to be a stay-at-home mom.

I'm so glad you're my husband, a man who honors his priesthood and does so much for me. Please be safe. Can't wait to hear from you!

Love you forever,
Hayley

Luke's Hallmark moment was interrupted by Dr. Allman.

"You know," he said, "the three of us here, together, sounds like the opening of a joke. 'A Baptist doctor, a Presbyterian dentist, and a Mormon reporter are on an airplane going to Africa." He paused.

"There's a punchline in there somewhere," Luke said.

9

Luke was ready for his first episode of *Suddenly Sudan*, which began with an all-day flight to Khartoum. He didn't especially like flying, but he had stocked up on dramamine. The plane stopped twice to refuel, once on the East Coast, and again in Belgium. Dr. Allman was nothing if not a gracious host. He thought of everything but the warm towels they hand out to first-class passengers.

Luke spent most of his waking hours reading from the Book of Mormon. To help pass the time, Dr. Franks began regaling Luke with dentist jokes.

"Did you hear that a study showed that dentists are the most likely to commit suicide? You know why, don't you?" Dr. Franks asked.

"I have a pretty good idea," Luke said.

"Because we're always down in the mouth," the dentist said. *Ba-rum-rump.*

Luke chuckled politely, but Dr. Franks acted like it was the funniest thing ever uttered by a human being. Unfortunately for Luke, it didn't stop there. Even Dr. Allman got into the act.

"What did the tooth say to the departing dentist?"

"Fill me in when you get back."

"What was the dentist doing in Panama?"

"Looking for the Root Canal."

"A patient goes into a dentist's office and says, 'Doctor, I have yellow teeth, what do I do?' The dentist replies, 'Wear a brown tie.'"

"Did you hear about the dentist who became a stand-up comedian? People just loved his biting satire."

It went on like this for a while until Luke could take no more and went back to reading the scriptures.

Upon arriving at the airport in Khartoum, it became immediately clear to Luke that they had entered a third-world country. The runway had a few potholes, and police or military personnel were everywhere. Luke noticed the arid conditions the moment he stepped off the plane.

Getting out of the airport was an adventure in and of itself. All travelers were required to check in with police upon arrival and state their purpose for being in the country.

After all that time on the plane, Luke felt disoriented. First, he figured out what day it was and the time. What he couldn't do was figure out the day and time back in Helaman, Utah.

Jimmy Mulliniks was the logistical coordinator for Samaritans Around the World and was based in Khartoum. He picked up the group at the airport and dropped them off at the hotel.

"I will pick you up in the morning. We've got a long day ahead of us tomorrow," Jimmy said. "Nine o'clock okay?"

"Yes, nine," Dr. Allman said.

Luke checked into his room on the 11th floor and tried to figure out what day it was. He turned on the TV and clicked through a couple of Sudanese channels before finding CNN International. He looked out the window and watched the bustle of the business district below. He pulled out his laptop, found a phone line, and sent an e-mail.

Hayley,

I made it! I'm here in a two-star hotel in beautiful downtown Khartoum. Aside from the black beetles I found in the bathroom upon my arrival, I'd say this is a perfect vacation so far. Thanks so much for your letter you hid in my bag. I have to say that's been the highlight of the trip. I can't wait to come home. But I'm also excited about meeting the people, especially the kids, here

and bringing a bit of joy to their lives. As soon as I find a calcu-
lator and figure out the time difference between here and
Helaman, I'll call you.

Love you forever,
Luke

After sending the e-mail, Luke heard a knock on his door.

"Dr. Franks and I are going down to the hotel restaurant,"
Dr. Allman said. "Care to join us?"

"I'm starved," Luke said. "I'm in the mood for Mexican. What
are the chances they serve Mexican food here?"

"About the same as the chances of finding Sudanese food in
Mexico," Dr. Allman said with a laugh. "They do have some
American dishes here, but let's live a little dangerously."

The restaurant featured people wearing a variety of clothing, some traditional, some modern. The women wore an outer
garment, called a taub, Dr. Allman explained to Luke. Taubs
covered the head and reached the feet. Some of the men wore a
long robe, called a jallabiyah, a skullcap called a taqiyah, and a
white turban called an imamah. Everyone in the place, except
Luke, was wearing sandals.

"Is it just me, or am I underdressed?" Luke asked his traveling companions.

This Middle Eastern garb gave the restaurant an exotic
quality. So did the menu, which was mostly written in Arabic.
Fortunately, the waiter spoke some English.

"What would you gentlemen like today?" the waiter asked,
adjusting his turban. "Can I get you some coffee or tea?"

"How about bottled water for all of us," Dr. Franks said.

"Luke," Dr. Allman said, "I want you to experience Sudanese
cuisine on your first night here. Will you let me order for you?"

"Can I trust you?"

"Of course. I think I'll order you ful. It's a main dish, and a
delicacy in this country. It's broad beans cooked in oil."

"My mouth is watering already," Luke said.

"We'll get a plate of goat and lamb, too."

"He needs to try karkadai, too," Dr. Franks said.

"What's that?" Luke asked.

"It's the national drink. It's made from hibiscus plants."

Luke wondered if drinking karkadai violated the Word of Wisdom.

He choked down his ful and Dr. Allman and Dr. Franks had some fun watching him do it. After a while, Luke felt a headache coming on. He hoped he had packed Tylenol in his shaving bag.

"How long does it take to get over the jet-lag?" Luke asked.

"About the time you'll be going home," Dr. Allman said.

Luke couldn't wait to lay down and get some rest. After dinner, he and his companions went back to their respective rooms.

"Get a good night's sleep tonight, Luke," Dr. Allman said. "You thought today was different. You're in for a day of culture shock tomorrow."

Dr. Franks laughed.

Luke collapsed on the bed and turned the TV to CNN International. *Where's Wolf Blitzer when you need him?* Luke wondered as he drifted off to sleep.

10

The next morning, Luke checked his e-mail and was happy to see a message from Hayley. He e-mailed her back, though he wanted to call her. Luke didn't though, not wanting to wake her up in the middle of the night.

Luke showered—Dr. Allman warned him it would probably be his last shower for quite some time—dressed, put on his beloved Mets ballcap, then carried his two bags to the hotel lobby.

He felt refreshed after getting a good night's sleep. He wasn't anxious to get back on a plane for a few more hours to southern Sudan, but he couldn't wait to get there.

"I don't want to scare you or anything," Dr. Allman said, "but this could be a pretty rough flight."

"Great. Now you tell me," Luke said.

"The Sudanese government has not approved our flight plans. We're going at our own risk. I remember a couple of years ago, the government tried to shoot down one of our planes. Another humanitarian aid plane crashed near the Nuba Mountains, not far from where we're going during this trip."

"Can't we drive to where we need to go?" Luke asked.

"Planes are not only the best way to get around, they're the only way, Luke. Because of this war, almost all of the roads have been destroyed and aren't suited for driving. Besides, this country is so huge, we'd lose valuable time getting from place to place. One thing we don't have a lot of around here is time. In my opinion, this is the worst humanitarian situation on earth."

"What's our itinerary going to be, then?" Luke asked.

"Well, looks like you're going to get a whirlwind tour of Sudan. First, we're going to visit a refugee camp filled with thousands of displaced people in eastern Sudan who are in the process of fleeing to Chad. We're going to the refugee camp first because there's a real emergency there. Hundreds of people are dying each week and they have next to nothing. After that, we'll go to southern Sudan, where we have a hospital with somewhat modern conditions. Then we'll go to a village in the Nuba Mountains. That should take care of the first week."

"I think you need a new travel agent," Luke quipped.

"Listen, I hope I'm not scaring you too badly. This is dangerous, but we've never lost a single member of Samaritans Around the World in the eight years we've been coming here. The Lord will be with us."

Luke never scared easily, but that was before he had settled down and married the prettiest woman in the world. Now that life was better than ever, it seemed all the more fragile. *Maybe I'm just getting old*, he thought.

In the lobby, the pilots were going over their maps and navigational charts. Dr. Allman and Dr. Franks were inspecting their medical equipment. Other volunteers were mingling together, discussing Bible verses.

Luke asked Dr. Allman and Dr. Franks why they participated in these humanitarian trips.

"The best part about this for me," Dr. Franks said, "is giving these people something to smile about. I don't see many smiles when they walk in, but after I finish fixing their teeth, they're all smiles."

"I do it because the best exercise for the heart is reaching down and lifting others," Dr. Allman said. "Let me tell you, I get a lot more from this than I give to the people. The first time I came here to Sudan a few years ago, I didn't know what to expect. The kids here are the future of the country. We must share with them the light of hope, or their future is hopeless. I love helping these children. They're so appreciative. I guess I could be lying on a beach somewhere or golfing. But I wouldn't trade this for anything. My wife is good to allow me to come here. The day after we get back, my wife and I will celebrate our 40th wedding anniversary."

"Congratulations," Luke said. "I hope I live that long."

"How long have you been married?"

"A little more than a year."

"Let's see your bride."

Luke pulled out his wallet and displayed the twenty photos he had in there.

"She's a beautiful woman," Dr. Allman said.

"You're a lucky man," Dr. Franks chimed in.

"Hopefully," Luke said, "my luck continues."

Jimmy Mulliniks and his staff showed up in a fleet of SUVs and took the group to the airport, where they boarded a large cargo plane-bound for the refugee camp.

"This plane weighs about fifteen tons," Dr. Allman said.

"Are we going to be able to get off the ground?" Luke asked, half-joking.

During the flight, Luke asked Dr. Allman to give him a little history lesson and background about the places they would be visiting.

"The Christians have suffered so much during this bitter civil war, some of it at the hands of the Sudanese government, which is run by Muslims," Dr. Allman explained. "At one point, the president of the country predicted Christians would be swept out of Sudan someday. The Muslims declared a jihad, or holy war, against the Christians. Still, the Christian church has grown despite the persecution. Problem is, there have been thousands of displaced Sudanese because of the civil war. The government has launched a campaign to rid the country of the Christians in the south. Unfortunately, that campaign is working."

From above the ground, Luke had never seen such an arid landscape. At the same time, he saw beauty in it. Sprawling along a large parcel of land was a makeshift village filled with tents and shanties.

"We're almost here," Dr. Allman said to Luke as the plane

dipped beneath the clouds. "When the refugees hear the sound of an airplane, it frightens them. They think it's another government-sponsored bombing. There are probably 10,000 people living down there in the most abject poverty imaginable. Basically, our mission is to provide medical assistance to a displaced population in this isolated region. We have enough supplies to care for 10,000 people for three months. We'll be keeping plenty busy."

"Where will we be landing?"

"There are no runways here, of course," Dr. Allman said. "All we've got is a dirt landing strip. It could get a little bumpy."

The pilots announced to the group to get into crash position—to bend over and place their hands over their heads.

Luke said a little prayer and the plane touched down with a loud thud. Though he wore a seat belt, he felt as though he was going to be thrown out of his seat. His head slammed into the seat in front of him.

"Hey, doc, I just got an idea for a new Disneyland ride," Luke said.

Dr. Allman laughed. "You've got a joke for every occasion, don't you?"

"I guess we'll find out," Luke said.

The first thing Luke noticed as he stepped off the plane was a stiff, hot wind blasting him in the face.

Quickly, the group began the unloading process. First, the volunteers drove a pair of yellow Humvees and a large truck out of the plane. "The Humvees will get us to where we need to go," Dr. Allman told Luke. "The truck will carry our supplies."

Then everyone began removing box after box from the plane. Luke jumped in to help. It was backbreaking work. Some of the boxes weighed hundreds of pounds.

"What's in this box?" Luke asked one of the volunteers. "The kitchen sink?"

"Close," he replied. "It's a gas-powered refrigerator."

"Why bring one of those?"

"We need this refrigerator for the vaccinations," the volunteer said. "We've got vaccines for measles, polio, and malaria.

The vaccines must be kept frozen or they will lose their effectiveness."

Luke learned the boxes also included emergency kits filled with surgical gloves, surgical knives, tongue depressors, disposable needles, gauze compressors, thermometers, and thousands of Amoxicillin tablets.

There were also boxes of therapeutic food for malnourished children to last three months.

"About one in five of these kids here are dying of starvation," the volunteer said.

A number of boxes, of course, contained all the toys and other items from the Helaman 6th Ward. And Luke couldn't wait to distribute those.

Some of the volunteers drove in the truck to the refugee camp, while the others followed in a yellow Humvee.

The refugee camp was right out of *National Geographic*. The area was lined with scant shanties made of sticks and tents. Thousands of gaunt, black faces turned out to greet the visitors from the United States. The vast majority of the refugees were women and children. Most of the men, Luke was told, had been murdered. Luke saw many young girls wearing braided hair and colorful beads around their necks. He also saw dozens of stick-legged infants too weak to stand on their own.

As they approached, the people began clapping and chanting.

"What are they saying?" Luke asked Dr. Allman.

"I think it's their way of saying they're glad to see us."

Many of the women were dressed in colorful garb—a stark contrast to their dry, drab surroundings. A long line of people snaked around a white tent.

"That's our little hospital," Dr. Allman said. "We'll give the shots there. There's another tent over there that will serve as a therapeutic feeding center for malnourished children. These children have witnessed horrific events in their lives. It absolutely breaks my heart. Those toys you brought will bring more joy to them than you realize."

Once again, the group unloaded boxes of food and toys and

other supplies from the truck and placed them in the humanitarian tents. Luke felt like he was going to pass out because of the heat.

After the work was done, Luke met the tribal chief, who had just finished burying a child who had died of starvation. He also met Emil, who served as a translator. Luke noticed a woman on her hands and knees, sifting through the dirt.

"What's she doing?" Luke asked innocently.

"Probably looking for food," Emil said flatly. "I want to thank you for coming. We are so grateful for your presence here."

Luke wanted to eat, but looking at the starving people, it was easy to ignore his hunger pangs.

Luke helped the men hand out food supplies, including rice and beans, to the people. As Luke would hand a man a box of rations, he would invariably say something to Luke.

"He thanks you," Emil said, translating his words.

Laboring beneath the scorching hot sun, Luke had never felt so useful or helpful in his life. He couldn't help but remember the scripture Hayley had quoted to him when she gave her permission for him to come to this troubled country.

"'. . . inasmuch as ye have done it unto one of the least of these my brethren, ye have done it unto me.'"

Those words echoed over and over in his head, humbling him deeply. He knew that coming to Sudan was the right thing to do.

Dr. Allman called Luke over to the white tent and he walked past hundreds of children, some being held in their mothers' arms. "Have you ever administered shots before?" he asked him.

Luke laughed. Dr. Allman was deadly serious.

"No," Luke answered. "I'm no doctor."

"We've got a lot of kids who need vaccinations. More than I thought. We need as many bodies helping as possible. That nurse over there will show you how to do it. Okay?"

"Okay," Luke said, "but won't we get in trouble with the AMA or something for this?"

"Luke, these kids are suffering. Out here, there's no such thing as the AMA. We simply try to do what our Lord and Savior, Jesus Christ, would do. And that's help these kids."

Luke had always been queasy around needles, but he couldn't worry about that now. A boy approached Luke and Dr. Allman, and Luke picked up the needle.

"This is going to hurt me more than it's going to hurt you," Luke told the small child, who couldn't have been more than five. He was frighteningly thin and looked like he would snap in two. His eyes were hollow and his cheekbones stuck out prominently. The nurse told Luke that the boy was an orphan whose parents had been killed in a bombing. On one level, Luke could empathize with the boy. After all, he had spent most of his life bouncing from one foster home to another.

Luke noticed there wasn't much skin on the boy's body. He gently stuck the needle in his arm.

The nurse watched to make sure he was doing it right.

"Good job," the nurse said. "Ready to fly solo? I've got a bunch of kids over here I need to attend to. If you have any questions or problems, just holler."

Luke nodded and motioned for the next child to step forward. *If only Hayley could see me now,* he thought. Luke wished that Hayley were there, not just for companionship, but because these people needed her nursing expertise.

By late afternoon, the lines had disappeared. Luke was exhausted in every way imaginable. Then he helped distribute the rest of the food to the people, who gratefully accepted it with a smile. Some hugged him.

"How do you feel?" Dr. Allman asked Luke.

"Tired," Luke said.

"Well, you may have helped save hundreds of lives today."

Later, Dr. Allman told the volunteers about the toys that Luke had collected in Utah. "Now that we've given those kids their shots," he said, "why don't we try to cheer them up?"

While Dr. Allman returned to the white tent to attend to the sick, the volunteers found the boxes filled with toys.

Dr. Allman had Emil call over the many children. Luke felt goosebumps cover his body as he handed out these small gifts that made the children's eyes light up.

He gave a stuffed teddy bear from the Fidrych family to a small girl whose forehead was covered with a large bandage. She smiled broadly as she embraced it and held it close to her face. He gave a Tonka truck donated by Bishop Law and his wife to a boy who looked at it in wonder and happily ran off to show his new treasure to his mother. To another child he gave a wooden paddle with a rubber ball attached with a rubber band, made by Brother Gruber. Children arrived in droves. When he looked into the children's eyes, he saw pain, hunger, despair. Luke looked for a package for the designated age and gender and watched each child open a gift. He gave a blanket knitted by Sister Sterling to the mother of a young infant.

This went on for about an hour or so, until every child he saw had a toy.

Seeing all of those Sudanese kids, Luke wanted more than ever to have children of his own. At that moment, he wanted to adopt every child in that refugee camp. He couldn't wait to write Hayley an e-mail and tell her about his incredible day.

Luke turned to Emil. "Do kids here like sports?"

"They don't play many sports," Emil said. "When you don't know where your next meal is coming from, that isn't high on their list of priorities."

"Guess I hadn't thought of that," Luke replied.

Opening another box, Luke took out a brand new soccer ball donated by the McMurray family. He put it on the ground and started kicking it around. Soon, he was joined by a handful of kids. Before long, they had set up goals and divided into teams. He couldn't understand a word they were saying, but their laughter he understood.

Luke decided it was time to teach the kids a game from his native land. He borrowed four bedpans from the hospital, then placed one on the dirt and marched off about 30 feet and placed another one on the ground. Luke turned an arid patch of desert into a baseball diamond, albeit in the rough.

By this time, many of the children had gathered around as Luke opened another box and pulled out a baseball, a bat, and about twenty gloves. The children couldn't figure out what this American was doing with such strange equipment. He gave his Mets cap to a small girl who examined every inch of it before putting it on her head, backward.

He asked one of the volunteers who was helping with the game to take pictures with the video camera.

Before long, Luke had instigated something resembling a baseball game, teaching the rules through Emil. What made it especially tough was trying to teach the rules to Emil first.

With his heel, he dug into the rock-hard dirt to create a pitcher's mound. Luke gathered the children together and showed them what to do. He threw the ball into the air and hit it with the bat. Thwack! Most of the kids oohed and ahhed as they watched the ball fly into the air and land in a bush some 100 feet away. A couple of kids chased down the ball, kicking up red clouds of dust. They wanted him to hit it again.

Luke divided the kids into teams, passed out gloves, and showed the kids how to put them on. He got emotional when he handed Brooklyn's old glove to the girl with the bandage. She placed the glove on her small hand, then picked up her teddy bear. Luke had her play shortstop.

Luke served as the pitcher for both teams. When he'd turn around to look at the players in the field, most of them were wearing their gloves on top of their heads. A thin boy about the same width as the bat he held, stepped to the plate.

"Get your elbow up," Luke called to him. "Emil, tell him to get his elbow up. His left hand should be on the bottom of the bat. You need to switch your wrists around."

Getting nowhere, Luke jogged to the plate to help him, then returned to the mound. After the first pitch, the boy offered an awkward swing. Luke went back to the boy. "Maybe you're a lefty," he said, turning him around, into the other batter's box.

Luke tossed an underhand pitch about chest-high and the boy uncorked a hit that sailed over everyone's heads and into a thicket in right-center field.

"Home run!" Luke shouted. "Ladies and gentlemen, the next

Barry Bonds! Kid, can I be your agent?"

The boy dropped his bat and picked up the crutches he had just received—the boy's leg was deformed—and Luke escorted him around the bases. The boy grinned and hobbled around the bases triumphantly.

After playing a few innings, he decided to give the kids some of the Munchak's food. A couple of kids tried some of the Munchak's patented wheat pudding. They immediately spit it out on the ground.

"I take it they don't like this stuff," Luke observed.

"They say it tastes like a vile weed," Emil said.

"Funny thing is," Luke replied, "people back home react the same way."

Luke found time to stop and watch the sun go down on the African plain. Full of hues of red, orange, and purple, it looked too beautiful, too perfect to be real, like a painting on a museum wall.

Dusk fell and the children returned to their homes. Luke went to a tent where he had a cot waiting for him to sleep on. He felt a little guilty sleeping there, rather than on the ground like all of the Sudanese people.

"Did you see that kid hit that home run today?" Luke asked Emil.

"That was a wonderful moment for him," Emil said. "He's an orphan. His father was murdered by the Sudanese government a couple of months ago. His mother was killed last week when she stepped on a land mine."

"Isn't there something we can do for him?" Luke asked.

"You already did," Emil answered.

The volunteers had pitched a few tents to sleep in. A million stars filled the sky and everyone was turning in for the night. Luke approached Dr. Allman.

"This might be a stupid question, but are there any phone lines here? I'd really like to call or e-mail my wife."

"You're right. That is a stupid question," Dr. Allman said with a chuckle. "The next chance you're going to have to communicate

59

with your wife will be at the hospital when we get there tomorrow."

There was so much to tell Hayley, but that would have to wait. He pulled out his laptop and began writing about his day. *Time and Newsweek will be begging me to publish this stuff,* Luke thought.

Dr. Allman lay down on his cot and exhaled.

"How did it go today?" Luke asked.

"I watched two children die," he answered somberly. "Where we live we are blessed to have technology and advanced medicine. Yet at times, I was powerless to help some of these kids. There's nothing worse than that."

Luke could barely move. Every muscle in his body throbbed. His stomach growled. But he had never felt more like a disciple of Jesus Christ.

11

The next morning, a few of the volunteers stayed behind at the refugee camp. Luke, Dr. Allman, and the rest of the group returned to the plane to go to the Samaritans Around the World hospital in southern Sudan.

"After this place," Dr. Allman said as the plane took off, "our little hospital will seem like the Mayo Clinic."

The hospital was actually a Christian church that had been bombed by the Sudanese government and then rebuilt and turned into a medical facility. It was staffed with twenty surgeons like Dr. Allman and all 100 beds were almost always filled.

Luke spent part of the day handing out toys to the children who lay in those beds.

"There are people in here who have walked for days to get here," Dr. Allman said. "It's about the only place to come for medical attention."

For many reasons, Luke had to admire Dr. Allman. Here was a truly Christlike man—a missionary surgeon who was willing to leave his comfortable practice in Dallas to administer to the sick and afflicted thousands of miles away in an embattled nation largely forgotten, or ignored, by the rest of the world.

As part of the hospital, which served as the social center for the area, Bible study classes were offered to restore hope to a hopeless people.

"We want to mend not only their physical wounds," Dr. Allman said, "but their spiritual ones as well."

Other classes were held for the large number of women,

where they learned personal hygiene and reading skills.

That evening, Dr. Allman showed Luke where he could find one of the few phone lines. It took a while, but when Luke heard the modem on his laptop connect to the Internet, he thought it was the sweetest sound he had ever heard. Finally, he was able to communicate with the outside world. He eagerly checked his e-mail and discovered he had twenty-one new messages. Sixteen of them were from Hayley and one was from Ben.

"I hate being a world apart from you," Hayley wrote. "But I know you're doing a wonderful thing there in Africa. Please, please, write as soon as you can. Love you forever."

Luke couldn't tie up the phone line for long, so he wrote Hayley a brief message.

I'm keeping busy, and safe, here. I can't wait to get home and tell you all about it. Know that I love you with all of my heart and that you're always with me.
Love You Forever,
Luke

The next day called for another flight. The humanitarian group left for eastern Sudan, to a village in the Nuba Mountains, near the Nile River.

"We'll be staying here for a few days," Dr. Allman said.

Luke asked Dr. Allman who the people were that lived there.

"More displaced people," he said with a trace of anger in his voice. "As if the situation wasn't dire enough in Sudan, oil found in the south has complicated these people's lives even more."

"What do you mean?" Luke asked.

"The government has used local militias to exterminate Christians—and anyone else living there—in order to maintain their oil-rich lands. They are pumping oil from their pipeline and will do anything to protect their interests. The vast amounts of money earned from the oil only leads to the strengthening of the military. The Sudanese people who have farmed land in the south for generations have been forced to leave. They have resettled in a marshland infested with mosquitos. Here, they feel reasonably safe."

But living in this swamp—the word Sudan is a derivative of an Arabic word, *sudd*, that means swamp—posed a host of other problems. Namely, diseases, like malaria, carried by the mosquitoes. Among the supplies being brought in by Samaritans Around the World was mosquito netting for the people. The mosquito netting had been dipped in an insecticide to curb the spreading of the fatal disease.

Also, the humanitarian group brought equipment that would help provide clean water—pumps, tanks, pipes, and chemicals for water-purification.

"Some of these people drink water straight out of rivers," Dr. Allman told Luke. "That causes a lot of cases of diarrhea and other problems."

Boxes were filled with tools and seeds so the displaced people could start their lives over again. Just like at the refugee camp, the Sudanese cheered when the Samaritans Around the World plane landed in the Nuba Mountains.

Within an hour of their arrival, Luke found people building grass huts with tools and planting seeds—all provided by Samaritans Around the World. Bibles were also distributed among the people.

"Why didn't we pass out food, like we did yesterday?" Luke asked.

"Tribal leaders requested seeds instead," Dr. Allman said, "so they can regain a sense of self-sufficiency. I'm constantly amazed by the strength of these people. Because of all the diseases, poverty, and war, the misery index is higher here than almost anywhere in the world. But the people forge on."

It must have rained three times that day. Unlike the refugee camp they had visited a couple of days earlier, drought was not a problem here.

That evening, Luke and the other volunteers once again distributed toys to the children. He never tired of watching the children open their gifts and paying him back with smiles.

12

That night, Emil burst into the tent occupied by Luke and Dr. Allman, shattering the pre-dawn silence and jarring them out of a peaceful sleep.

"Doctor," Emil said breathlessly, "a woman arrived saying her husband is badly hurt and needs medical attention right away."

"Where is he?" Dr. Allman asked.

"I do not know. The woman says she can take us to him."

Dr. Allman looked at his watch. It was nearly midnight. "Okay," he said. "Let's go."

"I'm coming, too," Luke piped up.

"You?" Dr. Allman asked.

"I'm no doctor," Luke explained, "but I'm sure there's something I can do."

Dr. Allman woke up Dr. Franks, and then grabbed his bag of medical supplies. Luke decided to take a bag with him, too. It was filled with a few priceless possessions—his laptop, his wallet with photos of Hayley, his quadruple combination, and a hymnbook. He did not want to risk having them stolen.

They all jumped into the Humvee and traveled down the pot-hole-filled road. Emil drove and the woman sat in the passenger seat and they headed into the darkness. All they could see around them was a giant sky filled with thousands of stars.

After about twenty minutes of driving, the woman became confused and started crying.

"What's wrong?" Dr. Allman asked.

"She says she does not know where her husband is," Emil said.

64

"So we're lost?" Dr. Franks said. "I say we get back to the hospital."

Luke agreed with that idea. He didn't get spooked easily, but he wanted to return to the refugee camp as soon as possible. Especially when Dr. Allman pointed out that the fuel light was on, indicating that the Humvee was nearly out of gas. Emil went to the back of the vehicle to retrieve a can of gasoline. But it was gone. Apparently, someone had stolen it.

As they made their way back to the hospital, the Humvee sputtered and coughed. Then the engine completely died.

"Does anyone know if we're in a Triple-A service area?" Luke joked.

"Looks like we'll be walking back," Dr. Franks said.

"We've got to find this woman's husband," Dr. Allman said. "But we'll have to return in the morning—presuming we make it back to our camp."

As the group began walking, all they could see in front of them was the faint light of the hospital in the distance.

Suddenly, from behind, they heard the sound of a truck. It approached them rapidly and pulled alongside the stranded Humvee.

"Who's that?" Luke asked.

"I have no idea," Dr. Allman said.

The pickup truck pulled in front of the traveling party and slammed on its brakes. That was followed by the sound of yelling and screaming. Five men wearing turbans and armed with AK-47s jumped out of the truck and began barking orders in a strange language. They shoved Luke and the others onto the ground. Luke hoped that they were being confused for someone else, that it was all a big mistake.

"Has this ever happened to you two before?" Luke asked Dr. Allman.

"Let's just do what they say," Dr. Allman said.

Luke didn't know who they were, but he surmised this wasn't the local Boy Scout troop. The men forced them to lie face down and spread-eagle on the ground. "If you get up," a voice said in broken English, "you will die."

"We're just doctors," Dr. Allman announced. "We're here to provide humanitarian aid."

Either the men didn't understand or they didn't care.

The men stood over them for several minutes, guns pointed at them. Luke noticed that the man watching Dr. Franks seemed especially nervous and agitated. He began arguing with another man and it soon escalated into a full-fledged shouting match. Sensing an opportunity, Dr. Franks slowly got on his knees and quietly began crawling away, unbeknownst to the thugs. Soon, Dr. Franks stood and began sprinting as fast as he could toward the hospital. Luke and Dr. Allman remained quiet, not wanting to draw attention to Dr. Franks. They silently prayed that he would be able to escape. That's when one of the men saw Dr. Franks running away. Angry, he jumped into the truck and pursued him.

"No! No!" Luke shouted and started to stand up. The man standing over him hit him in the back of the head with the butt of his rifle, knocking him back to the ground. Seconds later they heard a round of gunfire and saw Dr. Franks collapse to the ground in a heap. The truck stopped and the two men got out and shot the body three or four times, presumably to make sure that he was dead.

The men who remained fired a hail of bullets from their AK-47s, then placed their guns into the backs of Dr. Allman and Luke and shouted at them, as if to warn them that a similar fate would befall them if they tried to escape. The terrorists placed black hoods over the heads of Luke and Dr. Allman, then their hands were bound tightly with rope. They were forced to stand up, and then they were shoved into the back of the pickup truck. Emil and the woman were left alone. Luke clung to his bag as if he were clinging to his life. Then one of the men ripped the bag out of his hands. The truck sped off.

Not knowing what awaited them, Luke and Dr. Allman sat in the back of the truck, bouncing up-and-down over the rugged terrain. Wherever they were going, they were getting there fast, Luke figured. But he felt like he was going to pass out as he struggled to breathe under the black hood.

"I'm feeling light-headed," Luke told Dr. Allman.

"Carbon dioxide is building up," Dr. Allman said. "When you can, push the hood close to your mouth and exhale through it for fresh air."

For saying those words, one of the captors shouted at the doctor, then emphasized his point by slamming him over the head with the butt of a rifle.

Luke knew he had to be calm, to be in control of his thoughts. To survive, he knew he needed to act rationally.

They traveled in the truck for what seemed like hours. Luke kept hoping he would wake up from this nightmare. After they finally stopped, they were marched for several hundred yards at gunpoint until they were led into a building of some sort that smelled like a combination of urine and rotten food. Luke felt an arm grab him brusquely. He was taken down a dark hallway. Luke heard the sound of a door being opened, then he was pushed inside, where he was smashed into the wall and fell onto a cold, concrete floor. The hood was removed, then a man kicked Luke in the stomach before leaving and locking the door with bars behind him. Luke looked around the small, windowless cell.

At first, Luke began pacing, trying to figure a way out.

"Dr. Allman!" he shouted, hoping for a response. There was none. Luke had knelt down on the ground and bowed his head to pray when he heard the door open again.

In walked two men without turbans. One had a machine gun that he pointed at Luke's face. The other one did not appear to be armed. Both had dark facial hair. The one with the gun was a corpulent man and the other had a slight build. Both wore white cotton uniforms and black army boots.

"You will listen to me very carefully, or you will die," the smaller man said with a slight Middle Eastern accent.

"Remove your clothing and put this on," he said to Luke, throwing a white jumpsuit at him. Luke undressed as the men watched. They took his clothing.

"Your ring. Give me your ring," the man ordered.

Luke stared back at him. "Where's my bag?"

"What bag?"

"You and your friends took my bag. What did you do with it?"

"We do not have your bag," he said. Then the man angrily grabbed Luke by the collar and got nose-to-nose with him. "You don't seem to understand. You are not in a position to ask questions. Everything you have belongs to me. Give me that ring!"

Luke looked into his eyes and saw nothing but blackness and emptiness. If the eyes are the window to a man's soul, then this man seemed to be lacking one.

"Please," Luke begged. "Let me just have one thing. This ring is the only thing I have to remind me of my wife back home. Please. You have everything else. Can I just keep my ring?"

The man backed off and stormed out of the cell and locked the door again.

As the night wore on, Luke noticed it got progressively colder, to the point that he found himself shivering. Maybe it wasn't the cold, Luke thought, but the fear. He tried not to imagine the worst-case scenarios. He had heard of Americans being beheaded simply for being American. But he refused to dwell on that. He knew he had to be strong and maintain positive thoughts. He worried about Hayley. He wondered if he'd ever see her again. That thought only made him want to escape, but it was clear that would be futile, at least until morning. He worried about Dr. Allman, wondering how much a man who was nearly seventy could take.

Luke spent most of the night on his knees, pouring out his soul to his Heavenly Father.

Hours later, the same two men again entered his cell abruptly.

The one who spoke English approached Luke and promptly spit in his face. "You're being held in accordance with Islamic law," the man told Luke. "Tell me who you are."

"My name is Luke Manning. I am a journalist from the United States."

"You are lying!" he yelled. Then he turned and stepped out of the cell. The large man with a salt-and-pepper beard lumbered inside. He reared back and threw a punch at Luke's midsection

68

that threw him backward and knocked the wind out of him. Luke thought one of his ribs was broken.

"You really need to work on your interpersonal skills," Luke groaned as he picked himself up off the ground. Then the giant, olive-skinned bully began ranting at him in Arabic like a mad-man. Luke thought the man bore a striking resemblance to the Arnold Friberg painting of the wicked King Noah.

"Have you ever considered enrolling in anger management classes?" Luke managed to gasp, his body writhing in pain.

King Noah grabbed Luke again and threw a right cross at his jaw while the other man stood and watched.

"Now, maybe you'd like to tell us the truth," the English-speaking man said. "Tell me who you are."

"I already did. I am an American journalist. I came here to help the people of Sudan and write about it. That's all."

"We know you are an operative of the CIA."

Luke began chuckling as blood dripped from the corner of his mouth. "You think I work for the CIA?" he said. "Would someone who works for the CIA be dumb enough to allow his jeep to run out of gas in the middle of nowhere and be captured like this? I don't think so. The CIA guys are smart. I'm just a dumb journal-ist. Please, just let me and the doctor go. I have no information for you. I am of no worth to you. You seem like a reasonable man. Let us go and we'll leave the country tomorrow."

"Perhaps tomorrow you will be willing to tell us who you are. If you want to live, you will tell us the truth."

The men left, but an overwhelming sense of dread lingered in their wake.

Luke had heard of situations like this before, but he never believed he would find himself in one. He decided he would always maintain his dignity, no matter what his captors did. He knew the last thing he wanted to do was to show fear. He knew he had to earn their trust and respect somehow. That way, if he had to escape, or, heaven forbid, kill them, they wouldn't see him as a threat. If he could only establish a good relationship with them, he thought, as inconceivable as it seemed, maybe he could get out of this alive.

At the same time, being a journalist, Luke couldn't help but think about the great story he had—if he could survive long enough to tell it. He kept his thoughts on the future, on getting out, on being reunited with Hayley.

He determined to try to engage the captors in conversation. If he could built some sort of positive relationship with them, he figured it would be tougher for them to kill him.

The best way to stay alive was by cooperating passively, Luke thought. He knew the longer he could stay alive, the better his chances were of being released. As long as he stayed alive, he would be of value to these terrorists. He also knew he had to earn their respect by standing up for himself. Refusing to let them take his wedding band—he cherished that as a little victory. He removed it from his finger and read the words inscribed on the inside: "Luke, Love You Forever."

He prayed there would be more little victories in the near future.

13

After dropping the kids off at school, Ben headed to work. He had plenty on his mind that morning. One of his best employees had unexpectedly quit; a shipment of fruit from California was of very poor quality; and one of the checkers had come up $29 short the previous night. On top of that, Ben knew he needed to reorganize the Relief Society Presidency that weekend.

That night, he had a full schedule of bishop's interviews on the docket. There was the young couple that was having marital problems. *I'm no marriage counselor*, Ben thought. There was the young man in the ward who needed help processing his mission papers. Then Ben remembered a request from Sister Wilmsmeyer, who was starting a neighborhood book group. She had asked if he could approve their reading list for the year.

What's this ward coming to? Ben asked himself.

Ben locked his office door at the store, took the phone off the hook, and began reading the Book of Mormon, as he did every morning. He kept a set of scriptures there on his desk for that purpose. When he finished his reading, he dropped to his knees and rested his arms on his chair to pray. He found it hard to concentrate, though, with everything weighing on his mind.

When he stood up, he gathered up a folder filled with paperwork he needed to look over. There was a knock on his door.

"You've got a call on line two," the assistant manager told him.

Ben picked up the phone. "Kimball's Market. This is Ben.

71

How may I help you?"

"This is Reverend Thurgood with Samaritans Around the World."

Ben immediately dropped the folder, sending papers flying all over his office floor.

"I'm sorry to tell you we've had a tragic incident with our group in Sudan overnight," the reverend said. "Luke went with Dr. Allman and Dr. Franks, a dentist, to help someone. While they were gone, their car ran out of gas and they were ambushed by what we think were terrorists. The dentist was killed and Luke and Dr. Allman were kidnapped. Again, I'm so sorry. I feel horrible that this has happened."

Ben's stomach tightened and he felt like he was going to throw up. Nothing else going on in his life seemed important anymore.

"I understand you are a close friend of Luke's. You should be the one to tell his wife. Please tell her we are praying for her here and we are doing everything we can to bring Luke home. You need to talk to her as soon as possible because this is bound to be all over the news soon. Again, I'm sorry this has happened. I'm going to do everything in my power to bring Dr. Allman and Luke home."

Ben thanked the reverend for calling and hung up the phone. Nothing could have prepared him for this. This wasn't something that was covered in the Bishop's Handbook. How do you tell a woman that her husband has been captured by a group of madmen with little regard for human life? As her bishop, and her friend, it was his duty to tell her. He prayed for help to find the right words. While offering that prayer, he realized there were no right words to deliver such awful news.

Ben dialed Hayley's phone number.

Before he could tell her anything, Hayley said, "It's something about Luke, isn't it?"

"Yes," Ben said quietly. "I'll be over in a few minutes."

Those were the longest minutes of Hayley's life. Trembling, she unlocked the front door. Ben showed up wearing a grim face—a look that confirmed that her life was about to change.

Ben sat down beside her and took a deep breath.

"Hayley, Luke and Dr. Allman were kidnapped last night. Another man, a dentist, was killed. They believe Luke is alive. I'm sure they'll find him."

"I knew I shouldn't have let him go," Hayley said, sobbing. "Something told me this was a bad idea, but I . . . "

"Hayley," Ben interrupted, "I am so sorry this has happened. We've got to think positive. We will find him. You have to believe that."

"Who would do this kind of thing?" Hayley asked. "He was there to help people."

"Reverend Thurgood said they're not entirely sure who has done this or why. Luke and those doctors are heroes, as far as I'm concerned. Now, we're going to do everything in our power to get him home, okay?"

Hayley buried her face in her hands. Ben placed his hand on her shoulder while she cried.

"Would you like a blessing?" Ben asked.

Hayley nodded.

Ben called Brother Woodard and told him the news. Hayley's parents arrived in short order and embraced their daughter. Grit pronounced a blessing on Hayley, and then Ben offered a prayer.

When he was through, Ben looked out the window. "There's probably going to be a lot of media attention because of this," he said.

"It's probably best that we keep them away from Hayley," Grit said. "If we get questions, would you be willing to act as our spokesman?"

"Don't worry. I'll handle everything," Ben said. "I'll make sure you receive the private time you need right now."

When Ben got home, Stacie was watching the news. The lead story was on how a dentist had been killed in cold blood by Islamic militants and two other members of the group had been taken hostage.

"Luke's one of them, isn't he?" Stacie asked.

Ben didn't have to say a word. Stacie could tell by looking at her husband that it was true.

Ben then received a phone call from someone working for CNN, requesting a photo of Luke. He got one from Hayley and provided it to CNN. Within hours, it was being shown on every newscast in the civilized, and semi-civilized, world.

Word of Luke's capture spread quickly around Helaman, of course, and residents took it personally. That afternoon, when school let out, Boy Scouts dressed in full uniform and placed two dozen American flags on the lawn in front of the Manning home. Members of the Relief Society placed yellow ribbons on trees throughout town. Signs that said, "Pray for Luke," sprung up in windows of homes and businesses across Helaman.

Television trucks with satellites descended upon the neighborhood, lining the streets. Reporters set up their own little news bureaus and were filing reports every hour. They made themselves right at home, trampling flowers on their way to knocking on doors, searching for any scrap of information about Luke Manning.

By that afternoon, Grit called Ben. "You'd better come over to the house," he said.

Ben couldn't even find a place to park because of all the traffic. He simply left his car in the church parking lot and walked to Hayley's house. He was accosted by about a dozen reporters asking for a comment before he was able to slip through the front door. That happened again and again as members of the Relief Society dropped by, armed with food, though Hayley certainly wasn't in the mood to eat.

Soon after, Ben introduced himself and announced to the throng of news media that he would be making comments on behalf of the family. Ben later re-emerged to find a bank of microphones waiting for him on the sidewalk. He noticed that all of the TV cameras were on and rolling. He was nearly paralyzed with fear, but he had a job to do. He tried not to think about all of the people who would be watching him on TV.

"Ladies and gentlemen," Ben began nervously, "first off, I'd like to ask you to be as sensitive to the family as possible and respect their privacy. As you can imagine, this is a very traumatic and shocking situation. I'll be answering whatever questions I can. Luke's wife, Hayley, is understandably upset, but she has a strong faith in God . . ."

"How do you spell Hayley?" a reporter asked.

"H-A-Y-L-E-Y," Ben answered.

"What was Mr. Manning doing in Sudan? Did he know it was dangerous?"

"Yes, of course he knew it was dangerous. But if you know Luke, you know that he loves adventure. He loves helping others. That's why he went to Sudan. He put himself in a precarious situation because he wanted to help."

"Mr. Manning has a reputation for being a reporter who likes to do juicy stories," a reporter asked. "There are reports that Mr. Manning was actually in Sudan to do a series of stories on Islamic terrorists. Is that true?"

"Well, those reports are rumors. They're not true. Luke was there to cover the humanitarian work being done in Sudan."

"What's your relationship to Mr. Manning?"

"He's one of my best friends. As members of The Church of Jesus Christ of Latter-day Saints, I'm also his bishop."

"Could you describe Mr. Manning for us?"

"He's a funny, compassionate guy," Ben said. "He's happily married. He's only been married for a little more than one year."

"Will Mrs. Manning be available for questions?"

"No, I'm sorry. She will not be making any comments at this time. But she wanted me to express her gratitude to the community for the flags, the ribbons, and general support."

"Do the Mannings have children?"

"No."

"Can you tell us how she's holding up?"

"She's obviously very worried and upset. Like I said, they've only been married a year. They have a wonderful marriage. In fact, whenever they say goodbye to each other, they always say, 'Love you forever.' They know that no matter what happens, their

75

love will live forever. They believe that."

Then he announced that, in order to accommodate the masses, future news conferences would be held at the church.

"I'll probably be making further comments later today," he said. "Thank you."

Then he walked away from the microphones and into the house. Reporters shouted myriad questions at him at once. He ignored them.

Ben found Hayley's parents sitting quietly on the couch next to a phone that had been unplugged. "Where's Hayley?" he asked.

"She's in her bedroom, getting dressed," her mother said.

But Hayley remained in her bathrobe, sitting on the bed, not knowing what to think or how to act. All of her tears were dried up. She couldn't cry anymore.

Hayley stepped into the walk-in closet and she touched each one of Luke's shirts. A grimy pair of shoes he wore to mow the lawn lay on the floor.

Certainly, he was about to walk through that door, right?

Hayley turned on the computer and frantically searched for a new e-mail from Luke. There was none. She re-read Luke's message from the previous day. For all she knew, it might be the last.

I'm keeping busy, and safe, here. I can't wait to get home and tell you all about it. Know that I love you with all of my heart and that you're always with me.

Love you forever,
Luke

All of those years Hayley had waited to fall in love and get married in the temple. And now, her husband of one year was gone. "Why did I let him go?" she asked herself dozens of times every minute.

News reports stated that three Americans on a humanitarian trip in Sudan—a doctor, a dentist, and a journalist—had gone with a translator and a refugee woman to find the woman's husband. According to the translator and the woman, the dentist was shot and the doctor and journalist were taken away against their will. The translator and woman managed to walk back to the hospital to report the kidnapping.

Speculation from the CIA was that they had been abducted by radical Muslims who ran a training camp in central Sudan.

"They're a very dangerous group," a CIA spokesman said. "They've killed Americans before."

"What are the chances that he'll be released?" a reporter asked.

"Not very good," he said matter-of-factly.

Almost the entire country was captivated by this story. That night, Ben went to a local TV station in Salt Lake City because he was invited to be a guest on "Larry King Live," via satellite. Reverend Thurgood was also on the program.

Reverend Thurgood vowed to do whatever he could to help Luke and Dr. Allman. He said he was leaving the next morning for Sudan to speak to government leaders there.

Hayley watched the show as long as she could stand it. She couldn't believe they were talking about her husband on CNN. She regretted not seeing him off at the airport. She regretted letting him go at all. *What was I thinking?* she thought.

Pulling out the globe, Hayley stared at the country of Sudan for a minute, trying to guess where Luke might be. Minutes later, she logged onto the Internet and started searching for prices for an airplane ticket to Khartoum.

Hayley's mom knocked softly on the door. "Hayley," she said, "may I come in?"

"Yeah."

"What are you doing, honey?"

"Mom, I'm going to Sudan as soon as possible. Look, I can leave tonight and get to Newark International in New York. There's an Ethiopian Airlines flight that leaves at eight in the morning. It makes two stops, but that would eventually take me to Addis Ababa, Ethiopia, where I would switch to a Royal Jordanian flight that offers connecting service to Khartoum International Airport. I could be there in a couple of days. Only trouble is, I'd need to borrow $3,832 for airfare. Could you and dad loan me the money? Luke would die if he knew how much this will cost. Oh, and I guess I'd need to get a passport and visa . . . "

Then the absurdity of it all finally caught up with her. She pulled her mother tight to her and cried. "Oh, Mom, what am I going to do?" she said. "What am I going to do?"

"You just need to be strong," her mother replied, gently rubbing Hayley's back. "You need to rely on the Lord right now."

Hayley picked up a picture of herself and Luke on their wedding day—she in a beautiful white dress and Luke in a black tuxedo—standing on the granite steps of the Salt Lake Temple. Hayley lay down on the bed and clutched the frame against her chest.

She kept thinking of those three little words: Love You Forever.

14

Judging by the noise he heard coming from outside through the small cracks in his cell, Luke figured it was morning. He had survived his first night in captivity.

The brick cell was painted a drab brown color and was about eight feet wide and 10 feet high. He tried not to think about getting claustrophobia.

The men with the guns had taken away everything—his watch, his wallet, his pictures, his computer. But he still had his wedding ring. He knew he had to hang on to that, as tangible proof of his love for Hayley. Other than that, they had all but stripped him of his identity. He had no idea what was to happen next. Uncertainty was as much an enemy as the men with the guns.

When he was in college, Luke took some psychology classes. He had studied mental duress, never dreaming he'd be smack dab in the middle of a situation like this. He remembered the emotion pattern kidnap victims go through—fear, denial, withdrawal. Knowing those steps, he figured he could cope with the circumstances better. It provided him with a sense of normalcy.

Even still, Luke experienced a gamut of emotions, from frustration to fear. It was difficult to come to grips with the fact that his life was out of his hands. He knew he could die at any moment, at the whim of these madmen. He had no control over his present or his future. Maybe this was how it would end for him, he thought. His life with Hayley was over and he would never be a father. If death was the ultimate outcome, he could take solace in the fact that he had changed his life, become a member of the Church, and married Hayley. He knew that by marrying in the temple, his relationship with her would extend beyond the grave.

For the time being, Luke needed to maintain his sanity. He was a reporter at heart and he realized the scoop that he had. How else could he get this kind of access to terrorists? He knew he would have a good story once the ordeal was over. All stories have a beginning, a middle, and an end. In order to tell his story, he would have to endure and survive until the end. There had to be a future in order to tell the story and that helped keep him sane. He would remember details, remember feelings so he could write them down later.

Luke didn't know how long this would go on, but he was prepared for a lengthy stay.

He remembered reading about journalists who had been kidnapped. Even for those who didn't believe in God, being held captive was a spiritual experience. Luke felt a little embarrassed, though. There was something noble and courageous about being a reporter taken prisoner while covering a war. But he was there for a story involving humanitarian aid. What kind of a journalist was he?

He wondered if Hayley knew yet what had happened. If so, he imagined what she might be going through. Luke wished he could talk to her and tell her that everything would be okay. But that would be a lie. He didn't know how it would all turn out. No one but those terrorists knew what his fate would be.

Then he thought about that scripture he had read in Sunday School weeks earlier. The one about Joseph Smith being cast into a pit, into the hands of murderers. Suddenly, Luke could relate.

Where are the Three Nephites when you need them? Luke thought.

Luke thought a lot about Dr. Allman and Dr. Franks. He knew Dr. Franks was dead and he wondered if Dr. Allman was too. He tried entertaining himself with dentist jokes. He didn't find them any funnier this time around.

At that point, Luke realized his "mission" to Sudan may well extend beyond two years after all.

Luke was lying on the cold, cement floor when the slim man, the man who spoke English, entered his cell and ordered him to stand up. The bigger man with a beard, King Noah, stood blocking the door.

Luke remembered reading that the most important thing a civilian who has been taken captive can do is to engage his captors, to show them that he's human, not a piece of meat. So he decided to do his best to make an impression on his captors.

"Where's the old man?" Luke asked. "Is he okay?"

"You do not ask questions," the man said. "You are not allowed to ask questions."

"Sorry," Luke said. "I'm a reporter. I like to ask questions."

He was determined to get answers. Where was he? And who were these people who had kidnapped him for no apparent reason?

The large man pointed a rifle at him and marched him down a dark corridor. Luke tried to be as observant as he could of his surroundings. What surprised him were the many pictures of the Star of David with bullet holes shot through them. American and Israeli flags were painted on the ground—to be stepped on frequently. When Luke tried to step around them, the barrel of a gun was jabbed in his abdomen.

He was led down a flight of stairs and into a room with a table full of knives, swords, and machetes. Some of them, he noticed, were blood-stained.

"If this is one of those Ginsu presentations," Luke joked, "I'm not interested."

The slim man told him to be quiet. "You don't speak unless you are spoken to."

The men made Luke sit in a chair, where he was restrained with ropes. While the English-speaking man interrogated him, the other stood guard with a rifle.

"We know who you are," the man said.

"Who am I?" Luke asked.

"We know you are a spy working for the CIA of the United States government."

"I already told you," Luke said. "My name is Luke Manning and

I'm a journalist. The only thing I know about the CIA is how to spell it. I came to Sudan to write about the humanitarian service being done here among the refugees. That's it."

"You are lying to me," the man said, and then he slapped him. Luke thought of a perfect nickname for the man: Lucifer.

"I'm just a dumb reporter," Luke said. "What do you want with me? I'm of no use to you."

"Do you know what the penalty is for lying?" the man asked, pointing to the knives. "If don't tell me the truth, you will lose a finger—the one with the ring on it."

"I have no affiliation whatsoever with the United States government," Luke said desperately. "I can prove it."

"How can you prove it?"

"Check my computer. It was in the bag that you took. You can check all of my messages, in and out. You can read the articles I've written on there. I think you'll really like the one I did on this year's annual Helaman Days celebration. The mayor slipped in a pile of manure during the parade and Sister Fidrych won the pie-eating contest . . ."

"Shut up!" Lucifer screamed. "If you don't tell us who you are and who you work for by the time I return, your finger will be cut off."

That would really put a damper on my ability to type, Luke thought, hoping the man was bluffing. If they were trying to terrorize him, they were doing a pretty good job of it.

Then Lucifer walked out of the room, leaving Luke with the gun-toting behemoth, the one who looked like King Noah.

"So, King Noah, who do you think's going to win the Super Bowl?" Luke asked him.

Putting down his gun, the man approached Luke and began hitting him in the stomach and face.

This idea of building a relationship with my captors is really backfiring, Luke thought. The beating brought back memories of when he was a kid, when his father would do something similar to him after a drinking binge. But Luke had survived it then— he could survive it again now.

He watched the man pick up his gun. When Lucifer returned, he said something in Arabic to the guard, who untied Luke from the chair. He didn't know why and he didn't ask, either. He decided to follow orders. Lucifer and King Noah took him back to his cell.

None of this was making sense, he thought. For the moment, his cheekbone throbbed, his aching ribs made it hard to breathe, and he was weak from not eating. He touched his sore lip. It was bleeding. But he was simply glad to be alive, not to mention to have his finger still attached to his hand.

Hours later, his captors placed a hood over his head and forced him to another location. All he heard was men shouting and the sound of gunfire. Not exactly comforting.

Finally, after marching for about ten minutes, Luke was forced to sit down in a chair. The hood was lifted and he looked to his immediate left, where Dr. Allman sat. The doctor looked bruised, bloody, and disheveled, but he managed a smile for his friend. Luke was glad to see him again.

"I thought you might be dead," Dr. Allman said quietly to him.

"I thought the same about you," Luke answered.

"Do not talk to one another," Lucifer told them. Luke looked up and saw a video camera in front of them. All the men wore hooded masks and held guns in their hands.

"What is this, a photo shoot?" Luke asked sarcastically. "Make sure you get my best side."

A man clubbed Luke in the back of the head with the barrel of his gun. Dr. Allman instinctively tried to attend to Luke, but he was jabbed in the back with the same gun.

"Luke," Dr. Allman whispered, "knock off the wisecracks for once. You're going to get us both killed."

"You will speak loudly and clearly into the microphone and state your names," Lucifer told them. "Then you will read a message."

They were handed a piece of paper on which were typed the following words: "If the United States Government does not pull all of its troops out of the Middle East by the end of this week, we will be brutally executed at the hands of our captors."

So, Luke and Dr. Allman were pawns in an international stalemate.

Luke did as he was asked, but read the message as unenthusiastically as he could, with their captors standing menacingly in the background. The captors read their own message in Arabic, then shouted the same phrase three times: "Allah Akbar! Allah Akbar! Allah Akbar!"

"What are they saying?" Luke asked Dr. Allman.

"Allah Akbar," he replied. "God is Great."

Then the cameras were shut off, hoods were placed over their heads again, and they were returned to their respective cells.

Knowing Dr. Allman was alive gave Luke a measure of comfort. At least he wasn't going through this alone. When he was escorted to the bathroom—which consisted of a hole in the ground, Luke noticed some something written in the dirt.

John 3:16

It was a secret message left for him by Dr. Allman.

Luke knew the scripture because Hayley had made him memorize it. *"For God so loved the world, that he gave his only begotten Son, that whosoever believeth in him should not perish, but have everlasting life."*

Luke found a small stick and scratched in the dirt:

2 Nephi 2:25

It was the only scripture Luke could think of at the moment. *"Adam fell that men might be; and men are, that they might have joy."*

Luke knew that would keep the good doctor thinking. Maybe, if we get out of here, *I'll explain what 2 Nephi is*, he thought.

15

Hayley didn't sleep much those first few nights after Luke's kidnapping. She stayed at her parents' house and spent most of her time praying, pleading with the Lord to return her husband to her.

She spoke to Dr. Allman's wife on the phone, which made her feel somewhat better. She was the one person on earth who knew what Hayley was going through. They promised each other to stay in touch throughout the ordeal.

Hayley felt out of place at her parents' house, so she decided she needed to go back home. When she returned, she had to elude a number of reporters who were staking out her house. After walking inside the back door and locking it behind her, she hoped against hope that Luke would be there in his familiar spot on the couch, watching ESPN. To her bitter disappointment, the TV was off and the couch was empty.

Luke was not there.

Hayley entered their bedroom and was enveloped by the silence. She looked at the TV sitting on the nightstand. Her parents had kept her away from the television and the news and she had no desire to turn it on.

She called Ben and asked if he had learned anything new.

"No," Ben said, "not yet."

Ben had become a news junkie. For the first time in his life, he paid attention to every report from the Middle East, whether it had to do with Luke's kidnapping or not.

Later that week, Ben couldn't sleep, so he poured himself a glass of warm milk, sat down in the living room, and turned on the television. After a few minutes, the news anchor on CNN announced the breaking news of a video released by an Arabic TV station that showed the two kidnapped Americans.

Ben hurriedly called Hayley while an image of Luke reading a message appeared on the screen. Luke had bruises all over his face. He spoke slowly and without emotion. As bad as Ben felt, at least he knew Luke was alive. Then he noticed the figures in black standing behind Luke and the doctor, brandishing weapons.

"Hayley," Ben said, "you need to turn on the TV."

The news commentator translated the words of the masked terrorists: "We will subject these two men to the same horror that Americans have been inflicting upon our people for many years. If our demands are not met, these men will be executed."

The footage was shown about every twenty minutes and Ben stayed up for hours watching it, hoping to get new information. Hayley watched the report once and couldn't take anymore. She turned off the TV and went back to her parents' house.

The next day, ward members spontaneously held a ward prayer. They decided to announce it discreetly, through phone calls by hometeachers and visiting teachers. The last thing Ben wanted was for the media circus to follow them to the church and disrupt the ward prayer.

But in Helaman, it was impossible not to notice several hundred people in suits and dresses heading to the church on a Tuesday night.

Ben stood outside the main entrance and politely asked the news cameras to keep their distance and not to come in. He agreed to talk to reporters afterwards.

Hayley attended with her parents, but she didn't look well. During the meeting, she kept dabbing her eyes with tissue, trying hard to stay composed.

Inside the chapel, there were plenty of hugs. Tears flowed freely, especially as they sang a hymn to open the service.

God be with you till we meet again;
When life's perils thick confound you,
Put His arms unfailing round you.
God be with you till we meet again.
Till we meet, till we meet, till we meet
At Jesus' feet
Till we meet, till we meet,
God be with you till we meet again.

Ben said a few words, then knelt down and asked everyone in attendance to join him on their knees for a prayer. He prayed for Luke, for Hayley, for ward members. He prayed that the terrorists' hearts would be softened and that Luke would be able to return home soon.

Afterwards, as ward members left the building, Ben stuck around to answer questions, as promised. Their prayer meeting became the lead story on that night's local news telecasts.

As he was going home, guilt gripped Ben hard. Since he'd found out about Luke's capture, he replayed over and over again the conversation they'd had, about how great it would be for Luke to go to a third-world country and write about his experiences.

Was Luke gone forever, simply because of Ben's vain ambition? As his bishop and his friend, Ben felt personally responsible for Luke's predicament. He was devastated that he had put Luke in harm's way. He wished he had never had that idea. Ben knew he had to do something proactive.

Late the next evening, the phone rang at the Kimball house. Ever since Ben had become the bishop, there had been a steady stream of calls every night. Since Luke's disappearance, the phone never stopped ringing.

Stacie answered. "May I ask who's calling?"

"This is Senator Gary Trammell. May I please speak to Ben Kimball?"

"Um, okay, Senator, he'll be right with you."

She ran to the back of the house, where Ben was helping put the kids to bed, and held the phone up high with her hand.

"Can't you tell whoever it is to call back?"

"Ben," Stacie said, covering the mouthpiece, "it's the Senator!"

Ben gulped hard, took the phone, and walked into the bathroom.

"Hello?"

"Ben, Senator Trammell here. How are you doing?"

"Fine, thanks, Senator. How are you?"

"I'm doing well. I caught you on *Larry King* the other night," he said. "You did a fine job representing the Manning family, the State of Utah, and the Church."

"Thank you, Senator."

"I know you're going through a traumatic time out there in Helaman. I want you to know we're doing all we can out here in Washington to get Luke back home. As you may or may not know, I am a member of the Senate Select Intelligence Committee. The CIA is working feverishly on leads. Please pass along my concern to Luke's wife."

"I'll do that."

"Do you have any questions for me that I can try to answer?"

"Do you have any new information about where Luke might be and who might have him?"

"The CIA is still working on that. They are checking with their sources in Sudan and are doing satellite surveillance, looking for terrorist camps in Sudan. They believe Luke and his traveling companions may have simply been in the wrong place at the wrong time. Tell Mrs. Manning I'll do everything I can to help find her husband. I don't want to give you a false hope. The men who have him, according to our intelligence information, are extremely dangerous. They've killed Americans before simply for being American. When I find out anything more, I will be sure to let you know."

"Thanks, Senator."

Before the week was out, Ben also managed to talk to several other groups willing to help, from the Committee to Protect Journalists to the International Red Cross. They all sent letters to the government in Khartoum, beseeching its assistance in finding Luke. Publicly, the government said its intelligence services and police were cooperating and working on the case. But U.S. government officials and the media were highly skeptical of that rhetoric. The Sudanese government, after all, had long harbored and funded terrorism there.

The group that was providing the most help at the moment, Ben realized, was his own ward. He noticed members willing to help. They seemed to be kinder with each other. Nearly every family in the ward had signed up to provide meals for Hayley and her parents, extending into the New Year. Luke's kidnapping had brought the entire ward closer together in ways Ben never could have imagined. Every night, members would gather in a cul-de-sac near Luke and Hayley's house for an impromptu worship service or candlelight vigil in the cold and the snow. They would stand arm-in-arm in a large circle around an American flag and sing patriotic songs and church hymns. Then they'd just linger for an hour or more, talking, crying, and hugging. Any disputes or hard feelings that may have existed among them melted away.

In the truest sense of the word, the Helaman 6th ward was a family.

16

SOMEWHERE IN SUDAN, AFRICA

With each passing day, Luke felt like he was losing a piece of himself. He wouldn't let the terrorists do that to him, if he could help it. They could take everything from him—even his very life—but he knew they couldn't take away his faith.

Luke tried to mark the days as best he could. Doing so helped him to think of the world that existed outside his cramped quarters. But he lost track of time. Three days? Five days? Ten? He wasn't sure. His captors deliberately tried to confuse him that way, though, forcing him to stay awake for long periods of time by playing loud Arabic music on a radio.

He had a difficult time sleeping anyway, with a hard cement floor to sleep on, without a pillow or blanket. It was always cold and Luke could never get warm.

If I didn't know better, Luke mused, *I'd believe Jack Kilborn, or maybe my father-in-law, was behind all this.*

The captors fed him at odd hours, too. The food consisted of rice and little else. Though he was almost always hungry, he didn't like it when the food arrived because it would attract rats. He'd have to fight them off while eating. Every third day or so, they would give him a small piece of undercooked chicken, from which he was sure he'd contract salmonella. Or something worse.

The good news was that when it came to losing weight, this set-up was even better than the Atkins diet. *The way things are going, I'll lose this rain gutter around my waist in no time*, he thought.

Every once in a while, some men would show up unannounced,

open his cell, and spray him down with a high-powered hose. "What, no soap or shampoo?" Luke would ask them.

Luke pondered all the little things he missed—warm showers, ice water, shoes, blankets, books, his toothbrush.

What kept him sane was writing his story in his head. He didn't have a computer or even a notepad. Then again, he didn't need one. The sights, smells, and feelings he was experiencing in that cell were seared into his brain.

While writing his story in his head, he jokingly referred to his cell as the "Sudan Marriott." *The room service is lacking and the showers are always cold. Plus, there are no ice machines. Rating:one star.*

Mostly, though, Luke spent his time on his knees in prayer—hours and hours, in fact. He wasn't ever really sure of what day it was, but to him, every day was Sunday. He prayed for Hayley and everyone in Helaman. Of course, he prayed that Heavenly Father would bring peace into his heart and lessen his fears. For the most part, Luke did feel a calming peace that he knew could come only from the Savior.

Luke often lost himself in thoughts about Hayley, reliving over and over that last day they spent together before he left for Sudan.

He also started singing hymns aloud to himself. Not only did they bring him closer to Hayley, but, to his surprise, they were uplifting, too. As he sang, he imagined Hayley accompanying him on the organ. He dared not sing patriotic songs, thinking that the terrorists probably weren't big fans of "The Star Spangled Banner" and might shoot him on the spot.

Also to his surprise, Luke remembered more words than he could have imagined. As he warbled "Count your many blessings, name them one by one," Luke decided to try to find the bright side in his situation. It took him a couple of hours.

While he was on the second verse of "Come, Come Ye Saints," he heard a voice ask, "What is that infernal singing?"

Lucifer entered the cell. For the first time, he came in without the large guard. He appeared to be unarmed.

I can take him, Luke thought.

Then he realized that on a spartan diet of rice, he probably didn't have the strength to get out, even if he was able to pummel his captor for spitting on him, slapping him, and threatening to remove a digit from his left hand.

Instead, Luke figured this might be a good time to establish rapport with the man, as much as he dreaded the sight of him. He decided to try to engage him in conversation. As difficult as it seemed, Luke knew he had to try to turn this enemy into a friend. Or at least an acquaintance. As different as they were, Luke knew they had to have some things in common. He guessed that Lucifer was probably about his same age.

"It's called, 'Come, Come Ye Saints.' Where I come from, this song is really big," Luke said. "Say, you speak perfect English. Where did you learn it?"

"The University of Florida," Lucifer replied.

"You're a Gator, then."

"No. I never was. I never will be. I lived in America, it is true, but I hate America and everything America stands for."

"Certainly you must have gone to a few games at The Swamp."

"No. I did not go to college to watch your American football."

"What did you graduate in?"

"In economics. Summa cum laude."

"Impressive," Luke said. "So, what's a summa cum laude economics grad doing in a place like this?"

"You want to know why I am here? I will tell you. We are here to prepare for the destruction of all Jews and all Americans, praise be to Allah. Our day of recompense is coming swiftly. The United States of America and Israel will be destroyed forever, praise be to Allah."

"So this place is where you train for that?"

"Yes."

"Let me get this straight. You went to the United States, where the Statue of Liberty opens her arms to the weary, poor, and downtrodden, and you got a first-class education—only to later use that knowledge against us?"

"Yes. You could say that is a fundamental flaw in your system," Lucifer said with a wicked laugh.

Luke didn't like the direction this conversation was going, but he knew he needed to keep the man talking. It was great stuff for his book. On the other hand, if he got the man worked up into a frenzy, who knew if he'd take him back to the knife shop.

"How many people are being trained right now?" Luke asked.

"Too many to number. Hundreds."

"How old are they?"

"They're anywhere from age fourteen to twenty-one. They have enlisted to fight in this war against the devil."

Lucifer pulled out a cigarette and lit it up. "Do you smoke?" he asked.

"Only when I'm on fire," Luke replied.

Lucifer laughed. In fact, he laughed so hard that he began coughing. For the first time, he seemed almost human to Luke.

"What's your name?" Luke asked.

The man hesitated. "Khalid Abdullah Abdul."

At least Luke didn't have to keep thinking of him as Lucifer anymore.

"I'm Luke Manning," Luke said extending his hand. Khalid didn't move; he just puffed on his cigarette.

"Are you from Sudan?"

"I am from Saudi Arabia, a place that has allied itself with the devil, the evil empire of the United States. And you will die because you are an American."

"Have you, personally, ever killed an American before?" Luke asked.

"No," the man answered. "Not yet."

Then, just as abruptly as he'd arrived, he left.

"Nice talking to you," Luke said as Khalid walked away.

17

The American flags and yellow ribbons that filled Helaman buoyed Hayley's spirits, though she felt like she was living a TV "Movie of the Week."

After protracted begging and groveling by the media, Hayley finally conceded to conduct a short press conference. She read a statement, thanking all the people who were praying for her and her husband. She expressed her belief in God and His ability to work miracles, and then she closed by saying, "Luke, if by some way you can hear me, I love you forever." Hayley didn't answer any questions.

People around the country were touched by the tragic event and were amazed at how well she was holding up. In public, she knew she had to be strong and confident. In private, the tears flowed regularly. Everything reminded her of Luke.

One day, she received a package in the mail from Samaritans Around the World—it was a small box containing a few of Luke's personal effects that he had left behind, including his beloved Mets cap and the video camera. Hayley watched the video he had shot of the kids in Sudan and she bawled uncontrollably. Not only did she realize this might be the last time she would see her husband alive, she also was so proud of him and the work that he had been doing.

Hayley wanted to believe he was still alive. She wondered what he was eating, where he was sleeping. She wondered if he was hurt. Not knowing was the hardest part.

Several weeks had passed since Luke's disappearance and Hayley didn't leave the house much. She tried to avoid going out in public, simply because of all the people who wanted to talk to her.

Still, she decided she should attend sacrament meeting. That day, the ward had decided to hold a special fast for Luke. Hayley knew she couldn't lock herself up in her house all day, everyday. Besides, the news crews and reporters had left, going to chase the next big story. Mostly, she was glad about that. On the other hand, she took it as a sign that people had lost hope of Luke's return. No news wasn't necessarily good news. There wasn't a minute that she didn't spend thinking about Luke and what he must be going through a couple of continents away in a strange land.

In any event, she knew she had to go on living, even if that meant living without the one she loved.

Hayley began her fast praying, yet again, that Luke would soon return home. She knew it wouldn't be difficult to fast, since she barely ate anything anyway. She was constantly sick to her stomach. Every morning she'd wake up and make a trip to the bathroom to throw up.

At church, ward members rallied around Hayley, to the point that she felt somewhat uncomfortable. Not much was said to her, but almost everyone gave her a hug. After all the meals and other expressions of support, Hayley figured she had better stand, bear her testimony, and thank the ward. She vowed to herself to be strong.

When the time for the sharing of testimonies came, Hayley walked to the pulpit, wondering if she could get through it without crying. As soon as she looked out over the congregation, she felt tears spontaneously rushing down her cheeks. She grabbed a tissue from a box that sat on the podium. Before she could utter a word, she collapsed to the floor, nearly hitting her head on the corner of the pulpit. The congregation let out a collective gasp.

Ben and his counselors sprung up out of their seats and lay her flat on her back. "Dr. Zimmerman, could you join us up here, please," Ben announced into the microphone.

Dr. Z was already on his way and he attended to Hayley.

"She's fainted," he said. "We'd better take her to the hospital."

Brother Sagapolu emerged from the second pew and scooped Hayley up in his arms and carried her to her parents' car. Ben asked Brother Gruber to preside over the remainder of the meeting so he could accompany Hayley and her parents to the hospital.

Ben sat in the waiting area for quite a while with Brother and Sister Woodard.

"It's probably all of the stress she's been under," Grit Woodard said.

Dr. Z showed up and sat down in the waiting room. "You can go see Hayley now," he said.

"What is it?" Grit demanded. "It's the stress, isn't it?"

"I'll let her tell you," Dr. Z said.

Confused, Ben and the Woodards walked into Hayley's room to find her crying. Sister Woodard put her arm around her.

Hayley took a deep breath. "Mom, Dad," she said through her tears, "I just found out I'm five weeks pregnant."

Talk about bittersweet news. Ben was so thrilled for Hayley and Luke, but that joy was tempered by the realization that this baby may never know its father.

Hayley placed her hand on her stomach. "I guess that explains why I've been so emotional lately," she said with a faint grin.

"She had been fasting since yesterday," Dr. Z said. "That's not advisable for a woman in her first trimester."

Then Dr. Z looked at Hayley. "This is going to sound silly to you at a time like this, but for your sake, and the baby's, you need to avoid stress as much as possible. If you don't, there's a chance you'll have a miscarriage."

Then he turned to Hayley's mom. "Your job, Sister Woodard, is to make sure your daughter takes it easy. I can tell she hasn't been eating regularly. That's got to stop right now."

Hayley knew at that moment she had to be strong not just for herself, but also for the baby. She couldn't control what happened to Luke, but she could control the status of the little one growing inside her. As difficult as it seemed, she was determined to fill her mind with as many positive thoughts as possible. She could not allow herself to become engulfed by depression and despair.

Hayley's mom basically moved into her house and catered to her every need. Even when she didn't need it. Hayley was a strong, independent type, and being a nurse, it was hard for her to be the one on the receiving end of bedside manner.

Still, she allowed her mother to do all she could. It was nice for Hayley, too, because of her terrible bouts with morning sickness.

At night, when her mom was asleep on the couch in the other room, Hayley would shut her bedroom door and quietly sing hymns to her baby.

18

Teetering on the brink of insanity, Luke tried to manage his time as best he could by filling the endless hours with what he considered productive activities. Having a ritual to follow during the day put a sense of order in his life. When he wasn't praying or singing hymns, he'd do exercises, such as running in place. He knew he needed to maintain the best physical shape possible if a chance to escape ever presented itself.

As he pumped his legs up and down, he closed his eyes and imagined himself running up and down the streets of Helaman. He imagined seeing ward members and waving to them as he passed. When he finished, he felt tired, a healthy tiredness, not to mention a sense of accomplishment. "I bet I ran about four miles today," he'd proudly say to himself, panting.

Luke found other ways to keep himself busy, such as replaying famous games he could remember. He spent a couple of hours recreating the 1986 World Series between the Mets and Red Sox, with a running commentary by Vin Scully. He pitched an imaginary ball, swung an imaginary bat, ran imaginary bases, sold imaginary peanuts in the stands. When guards passed by, they looked at him like he was, well, nuts. His favorite part was the recreation of the ball rolling between Bill Buckner's legs. He even did instant replays in slow motion.

Still, he felt so alone. He got so lonely that he even missed his father-in-law.

Luke looked forward to his daily trips to the bathroom because it allowed him to get out of the fetid cell. Besides, he couldn't wait to see what message the doctor had left him. Not only were they inspirational, but sometimes they were like a puzzle that kept him guessing. One day he saw the letters "KTF." It took him all day to conclude that the acronym stood for "Keep The Faith."

So Luke scratched into the dirt his own acronym: "CTR."

That'll keep the doctor guessing, Luke thought.

One night, while he was on his way to the bathroom, accompanied by an armed guard, Luke heard a man yelling and running toward him. The captor with the gun seemed surprised and confused as the man drew a small knife and plunged it into Luke's thigh.

Luke shrieked in pain, then hit the ground, unconscious. The terrorists scrambled frantically and apprehended the assailant. They carried Luke to a small room with a box of medical supplies.

Blood poured from Luke's leg. Within minutes, Dr. Allman was escorted into the room by the captors. Seeing it was Luke, he quickly went to work while three captors with guns stood around him, watching. Dr. Allman stanched the bleeding by putting his hand on the wound. Then he grabbed the hand of one of the captors, placed it on Luke's wound, and searched in boxes for needle and thread to sew it up. He completed the surgery in about half an hour. By the time Dr. Allman had tied the last knot, Luke briefly regained consciousness.

"You're going to have a nasty scar," Dr. Allman said to him. "But you'll be fine, my friend. God bless you."

With that, they took Dr. Allman back to his cell.

When Luke came to, he was lying in his cell. The pain in his leg was intense and he could barely move. He uttered a mild curse word to himself.

"Luke," said a child's voice.

Surely, I must be dreaming, he thought.

"Do I need to get out the swearing jar again?" the voice said.

Luke squinted and saw a small figure, bathed in light, sitting cross-legged against the wall.

How could it be? Luke thought. *Am I dreaming? Am I hallucinating? Am I dead?*

"You shouldn't talk like that, you know," said the voice.

"Brooklyn?"

"Oh, good," Brooklyn replied. "I was afraid you might not remember me."

"What are you doing here? You're . . ."

"Dead?"

"Yeah."

"Yes, I'm dead, but only physically," the girl said.

"Does that mean I'm dead, too?"

Brooklyn glanced around at his cell. "For your sake," she replied, "I hope not. I wouldn't want to be stuck here forever."

"I'm still alive?"

"Of course. You still have a lot of other things to do in life before you go home."

"When you say home, do you mean an earthly home? Or a heavenly one?"

"Both."

"What do I still I have to do?" Luke asked.

"I'm not supposed to say," Brooklyn said. "It's against the rules."

"You need to be careful," Luke said, looking at the cell door. "They might see you."

"Don't worry. They can't see us. Only you can. Besides, even if they could see us, what could they do?"

"Us?" Luke asked. "Who's us?"

Then he noticed another figure next to Brooklyn. She was another young girl, about Brooklyn's age, with puppy-dog eyes, long eyelashes, and auburn hair.

"Who's this?" Luke asked.

"This is my friend, Esther. I was never able to go on a mission, so I guess you could say she's like my companion. We're always together."

"Hi, Esther," Luke said. The girl smiled.

"Why doesn't she say anything? Maybe, being with you, she can't get a word in edgewise."

Brooklyn laughed. "She's not allowed to talk."

"Why?"

"It's just part of the rules."

"Rules? Why do you keep talking about rules? What rules?"

"We have rules in heaven, you know."

"I was afraid of that," Luke said. "What's heaven like, anyway?"

"A lot nicer than this."

"What do you do up there? Are there really people floating around, playing the harp?"

"No. I haven't had any harp lessons. We have more important things to do. We do a lot of checking on what's going on down here on Earth. Esther and I saw you get baptized. We saw you marry Hayley in the temple. That was really neat. A lot of us were happy about that. Your mom sure was."

"My mom? You've seen my mom?"

"Of course. She's very nice. She wanted me to say hi to you and tell you she loves you. She couldn't come because . . ."

"Don't tell me. Rules?"

"Yeah."

"Please say hi to my mom for me, okay."

"I will. Esther and I saw you give my baseball glove away a little while ago."

"Hope you don't mind."

"Why would I? It's not like I can use it anyway. At least you made those kids happy."

"Is my life going to be over soon? Is that why you've come to me?"

"It's not your time yet. That's why I was sent here, to give you that message."

"Who sent you?"

"Who do you think? You know—the one you've been praying to for hours and hours and hours every day. All the people back home are praying for you night and day, too. I guess there were so many prayers that He thought he'd better send someone to brighten your day."

"Well," Luke said, "you have. Thank you."

"We've got to go. You just need to endure to the end. Think of this as an extra-long time out."

Brooklyn and Esther faded away. Luke lay his head down and fell asleep.

When he awoke again a couple of hours later, he looked all over his cell.

"Brooklyn, come back," Luke said. "Please come back."

Luke reflected on his conversation with Brooklyn. "Boy, this solitary confinement thing is taking a toll on me," he said to himself.

"Who are you talking to?" asked Khalid as he opened the door.

"Myself," Luke replied.

"We thought you might die. But you did not," Khalid said.

"Disappointed?"

"The man who stabbed you did it on his own. He was misguided. He thought he was doing Allah's will. He did not realize that you are of some value to us. There will be plenty of time later to kill you. Besides, I'm glad you'll be living a little longer. I enjoy speaking English with an American again."

"Happy to be here for your enjoyment. Could you at least let me thank Dr. Allman for saving my life?"

"You cannot."

"Figures. What should I have expected from an Islamic radical?"

"You cannot thank the doctor because he is dead."

Luke sat in shock, letting the terrible news sink in. "Why did you kill him?" he asked angrily.

"We did not kill him. We found him dead in his cell. Might have been a heart attack."

"Can't imagine why," Luke said sarcastically. "Keeping a seventy-year-old man, an innocent man, in conditions better suited for animals—who would have thought he could die?"

Khalid was becoming agitated. Luke tried to move his leg and groaned in pain.

The irony was not lost on Luke, that he was the one who had

almost died, probably should have died, if not for Dr. Allman. Why did Dr. Allman have to die while he still lived? He wished Brooklyn were still around so he could ask her that question.

19

As Christmas approached, kids waited in line to sit on Santa Claus' lap at Kimball's Market. At church, they acted out the Christmas story. At home, they decorated trees. And their parents stressed out about shopping and bills.

Yet Christmas wasn't the same around Helaman. Amid the peace and joy of the season, there was gloom and sadness. Because of all of the snow, the American flags which had adorned the streets of Helaman the first couple of weeks after Luke's disappearance had been folded up and placed in storage. The signs of support that hung in windows had ripped and faded. Yellow ribbons that had hung on trees had blown away. Media crews that had camped in front of Hayley's home had packed up and gone.

In many ways, Hayley and the rest of the town were glad to be rid of those vulture-like reporters. But they realized that when they were gone, it meant no coverage of Luke's kidnapping. It was a sign that it had gradually slipped from public consciousness.

Christmas night, while Ben and Stacie were putting the kids to bed and cleaning up dishes from the dining room table and wrapping paper off the floor, they heard a special report coming over the television.

"Terrorists claim to have killed Dr. Owen Allman, a man who was abducted while on a humanitarian trip in Sudan six weeks ago. They said the Dallas, Texas doctor's murder was retribution for the deaths of Muslims all over the world caused by the

United States. They also said they will soon kill another man they have been holding hostage, Luke Manning, from Helaman, Utah, if their demands are not met."

The photo of Dr. Allman's lifeless body was shown on the Internet.

While Ben tried to get a hold of Hayley and her parents— the phone line was busy—Reverend Thurgood came on TV for a live interview. He had gone to Sudan to request help from the Sudanese government, but to little avail. On TV, Reverend Thurgood condemned the killing and praised the life of Dr. Allman. "It's so senseless," he said, "to kill such a good man as Dr. Allman."

The news showed footage of a distressed Mrs. Allman, who would not be celebrating her 40th wedding anniversary with her husband.

Reverend Thurgood also made a plea to the terrorists for Luke's safe return.

Hayley didn't sleep or eat much for days after that. She placed a call to Mrs. Allman to express her condolences. At least Mrs. Allman knew that her husband was in a far better place.

Hayley's condition worsened over the next week or so. She was hospitalized and the doctors were concerned that she would lose the baby due to all of the stress. They put her on sedatives in hopes that it would allow her to rest and take her mind off the events in Sudan.

While Hayley was in the hospital, Senator Trammell, who was in Utah on Christmas vacation, visited her secretly, without an entourage of reporters. "Be strong and take care of that baby," he told her. "We're doing everything we can to bring your husband back to you."

Afterwards, Ben pulled the senator aside. "Is there anything new you can tell me?"

"I spoke to the CIA director before I came to Utah," he said. "Don't say anything to anyone about this, but now that Dr. Allman is dead, the CIA doubts Luke will last much longer, either. These animals will only spare Luke's life if our government removes all of its soldiers from the Middle East. You know and I know that's not going to happen. The good news is we've got the CIA, the FBI, and the military working on the case, trying to find out who exactly has done this and where they are."

"Isn't there anything we can do?" Ben asked helplessly.

The senator shook his head. "Just keep praying for him," he said.

20

Based on their conversations, Luke felt that he was beginning to endear himself to Khalid. It had been days since his life had been threatened. Maybe being stabbed in the leg turned out to be a good thing after all. If nothing else, it had bought him some time.

Luke could finally stand up again and hobble around his cell. But he didn't want his kidnappers to know that. He wanted them to keep thinking that he was an invalid—too injured to be an escape threat.

Khalid stopped by regularly. Once, he brought a kettle and two cups with him.

"I have brought you tea," he told Luke. "It will help your leg heal."

Luke was surprised by the man's apparently kind gesture. He didn't want to offend him declining the invitation, but he knew he had to.

"Thanks," Luke said, "but I don't drink tea."

Khalid looked at him strangely as he poured himself a cup. "I just told you, this tea will help your leg heal."

"I appreciate the gesture," Luke said, "but I'll be fine without it."

Luke decided to loosen him up again. After all, he prided himself on being an expert interviewer and conversationalist.

"Could I have my wallet?" he said. "It's in my bag. I'd really like to see the pictures of my wife. I'm sure that will help my recovery. Khalid, you must have a wife . . ."

Khalid bent down where Luke lay and stuck a finger in his face. "Don't you ever call me by that name," he said.

"Okay," Luke replied. "You must be married. Don't you think about your wife?"

There was no reply. Khalid simply stared at the wall.

"Do you have children?"

"Yes, I have a wife and children. I have not seen them for many months."

"Are they in Saudi Arabia?"

"That is not of your concern."

"My wife and I hope to have children someday," Luke said.

Suddenly, Khalid removed Luke's wallet from his own pants pocket.

"My wallet!" Luke said. "May I have it?"

"This is your wife?" Khalid asked, pointing to a snapshot of Hayley.

"Yes."

"She is a beautiful woman."

"Yes, she is. And more than anything, I want to see her again. She means everything to me. I love her with all of my heart. No one should be held against his will, separated from the one he loves, right?"

"You will never see her again."

Luke couldn't allow Khalid to rattle him.

"So, what are your plans with me?"

"If your government does not meet our demands soon, you will be executed. Someone must pay for the sins committed against Allah's people."

"Sins?"

"Yes."

"I respect your religion," Luke said. "I know you believe in the Quran. Doesn't it speak of love? Of peace? Doesn't Islam condemn the shedding of innocent blood?"

"Have you ever read the Quran?"

"No," Luke admitted. "Not all of it. Just bits and pieces."

"Then do not seek to lecture me about the Quran. It is a book

108

filled with poetic verses that are not understood to all men. What we do is the will of Allah. It is our mission to fight for the oppressed who cannot fight for themselves."

"How do you plan to do that?" Luke asked.

Khalid flashed a malevolent grin. "Death and chaos," he said. "Suicide bombings. Chemical weapons. Biological weapons. There are many like me who are already in the United States, hiding and waiting for the perfect moment to attack. They are carefully plotting and planning, and your police and military and government have not a clue."

Luke felt chills go up his spine. Back home, he thought, most Americans were living their lives, blissfully unaware that hundreds of men were working feverishly, day and night, preparing for their destruction.

"We have thousands of men all over the world who are trained to kill and destroy. They are trained to hijack airplanes, buses, and trains. They are taught to plant explosives and blow up cities the size of New York and Los Angeles. They're all volunteers, all working for Allah."

As disturbing as this information was, Luke knew he had an exclusive interview with a terrorist. It would be great stuff for his book. Luke tried to be as unemotional and objective as he could be.

"How is this kind of training done?" Luke asked.

"They are taken up in an airplane and told to jump out. They do not know if their parachute will work or not. But they jump, because they are told to. It boosts their confidence. I teach English to those who are being dispatched to America. After training, volunteers are split up into groups. We provide them with fake passports and visas to wreak havoc and terror on Americans and Jews. The man who runs this camp boasts to his trainees of the killings of Americans and Jews that he has been involved in. He is proud of the fact that the FBI lists him among the Ten Most Wanted in the world."

"I notice you refer to these people who are being trained as 'they.' Why did you enlist for this? With all due respect, you seem like a reasonable man."

"You Americans do not understand," Khalid said, his voice rising. "You are too proud, too ignorant of the plight of the Muslim people. You do not understand the anger, the rage that exists in the hearts of my people. You Americans have bred this anger, through your policies and actions. You have trampled on holy land because of your greed and your lust for power. This will come back to you one hundred fold in the form of a holy war filled with violence and destruction. Blood will flow through your streets. Your people will wail in the streets, mourning the loss of thousands. Then you will begin to understand what my people have been suffering for generations."

For the next twenty minutes, Khalid outlined in graphic detail the history of the United States' relations with the Arab world.

"You certainly know your history," Luke said.

"The history I learned at the University of Florida was a warped, American version. It was not correct," Khalid explained. "And while I was in the United States, I saw first-hand your greed and your opulence, your desire to oppress my people. You Americans export your McDonald's, your Coca-Cola, your Cadillacs, your Hilton Hotels, your Michael Jacksons . . ."

"Wait, as an American, and I think I speak for all Americans here, we don't want to be blamed for Michael Jackson, okay? We don't claim him as one of our own."

"Your lifestyle is not in harmony with Mohammed's teachings. America follows the devil. You must be swept from the earth."

"Why do you hate us so much?"

"I believe I just explained why."

"No, I mean why do *you* hate us."

Khalid sat down in the cell across from Luke and looked around nervously, as if he didn't want to be seen.

"When I was a boy, my uncle was like a father to me," he said. "My father died before I was born. My uncle played soccer with me and taught me many things. One summer, he traveled to Lebanon for work. While he was there, Israeli jets, without provocation, attacked the apartment building he was in, killing my uncle and thousands of others, including women and children. In the United States, the attack went without notice or concern. In fact, your money and political power caused it to happen. You ask me why I hate your country, I tell you it is because I hold it responsible for the murder of my uncle. Your country will pay the price. His death is on the heads of the Americans. When I was older, I was recruited, along with many others, to take up the cause of this jihad against America and all it stands for."

"Doesn't America stand for anything good to you?" Luke asked. "When you were in the United States, as a Muslim, weren't you free to pray and worship in the way of your choosing? Why would you deny others the same right and privilege?"

Khalid stood up, stormed out of the cell, and did not return for many days.

21

HELAMAN, UTAH, USA

Every morning, Ben awoke with an overpowering sense of dread. Doubt frequently crept in. He could only imagine what it was like for Hayley. And Luke.

Ben knew he wasn't supposed to feel this way, especially being a bishop. Especially with ward conference coming up. He had received the topic of the conference from the stake president: hope and faith.

Ben constantly felt his faith wavering. It seemed whenever he allowed himself to believe that Luke would be returning home soon, the reality of what Senator Trammell had told him over-shadowed his faith. Those people just didn't let American hostages go out of the goodness of their hearts. They were nefarious characters who killed Americans for no other reason than being American.

The only antidote for his troubles was constant prayer. Ben prayed for strength and for inspiration. How could he impart a powerful talk on faith if his own faith was faltering?

While Ben was in the shower, he decided to skip work. He called the assistant manager to gave him some instructions and told him that he would be out until the following day.

Stacie was a little more than concerned when Ben told her he was going to take a drive up Provo Canyon instead of going to the store.

"Why are you going there?" she asked.

"I've got an appointment."

"An appointment? In the canyon? Who on Earth are you going to talk to in the canyon?"

"It's not exactly anyone on Earth."

Stacie understood.

"Do you have your cell phone with you, in case I need to get a hold of you?"

"Yeah," Ben said. "I should be back by dinner time."

Ben left his car in an empty parking lot not far up the canyon. He zipped up his coat, tied his boots, placed his keys and his quadruple combination in a backpack, and began hiking up a narrow trail.

There was something about being all alone in the mountains that helped Ben feel close to God. While hiking, he poured out his heart in prayer. When he arrived, out of breath, at the top of the mountain, Ben gazed out over the sprawling Utah Valley landscape. With that perspective, he felt like he could see things clearly, closer to the way the Lord sees them.

Ben brushed the snow off of a rock and sat down. He spent two hours looking up every scripture containing the words "hope" and "faith" in the standard works. While he felt encouraged by those passages, there didn't seem to be anything new, nothing that he didn't already know. It was funny, he thought, that while faith was the first principle of the gospel, it was often considered basic and frequently skipped over or ignored. So why was he having such a difficult struggle with it?

Ben closed his scriptures and looked up at the sky. "What would Thou have me speak about?" he asked. "Please help me."

His backside sore from sitting on the jagged rock for so long, Ben stood and began trudging around in the snow.

By the time Ben checked his watch, he saw it was already late afternoon. The sun was quickly setting and he decided he had better head home. While he had enjoyed his time meditating in the mountains, he was disappointed, too. He had truly believed that the Lord would write his talk for him. He realized he had no better idea of what he was to speak about than he'd had when he arrived.

Ben reached into his backpack for his car keys. He removed his scriptures and shook the backpack and dumped it upside down. It was empty. He felt his pants pockets and his coat pocket. No sign of the keys. Panic washed over him. Visions of dying of hypothermia or frostbite crossed his mind. The cold hadn't bothered him up to that point, but now he was starting to notice it. And it was getting colder.

He retraced his steps, following the footprints in the snow and looking carefully for anything shiny. It was nearly five o'clock and dusk was falling. He knew it would be difficult to make his way down the steep trail in the dark. Stacie would start to worry, so he pulled out his cell phone.

"Service unavailable," it read.

As if he didn't have enough problems. He imagined the news reports:

"An LDS bishop was rescued by helicopter tonight at enormous taxpayer expense after he lost his keys in the mountains above Provo. More at ten!"

Ben cringed, imagining what the Boy Scouts would think. The previous summer, he had lectured them all about never going into the woods alone.

"An LDS bishop had three fingers and two toes amputated after he skipped work and wandered around in the mountains alone all day. Doctors say he may never work a cash register again."

He would bring shame to his family, his ward, his town, his Church.

"An LDS bishop died last night after being stranded on a mountain overnight while trying to prepare his talk for ward conference."

Ben knelt down in the freezing snow and offered a simple but heartfelt prayer. "Please, Father," he said. "Let me find my keys. I know Thou hast all power and canst do all things. Please, help me find them."

When he stood up, he wondered if he had locked the keys in the car. He thought about going back down the mountain. After all, he had gone over every square inch of that mountaintop looking for those keys.

Just as he started back down the trail, he looked down and, right there at his feet, lay his keys. Ben dropped back down to his knees and thanked Heavenly Father. Then he happily followed the trail to the parking lot.

Safe and warm in his car, with the heat cranked up, Ben was puzzled. He swore he had walked over that patch of snow three or four times. So why didn't he see his keys? He knew it wasn't dumb luck or his own ineptitude that allowed him to find them. The answer came to him as clear as a spring day. His talk wrote itself while he traveled back down the canyon.

Ben didn't sleep much Saturday night. He felt good about his talk, but he was nervous. He hoped he could deliver it in a way that was pleasing to the Lord. Not to mention the stake president.

At ward conference, when it was Ben's turn to speak, he stepped to the microphone and told about his experience in the mountains earlier that week.

"It's kind of a funny story, now," Ben said. "While I was up there, looking desperately for my keys, nothing was more important to me than those keys. To me, being able to find those keys was a miracle. When we think of miracles, we tend to think of Moses parting the Red Sea or Jesus walking on water. But can't the Lord, who effected those miracles centuries ago, perform miracles today, both large and small? The sun comes up every morning. Isn't that a miracle? Without even thinking about it, we breathe in thousands of times a day and He provides the air. Isn't that a miracle? Don't we believe He still lives? Don't we believe He loves us and watches over us? Then why is it so hard for us to believe that He can do anything on our behalf, so long as we have hope, and faith, in Him? It is my testimony that the Lord can work mighty miracles in our lives, if we allow Him to."

Then he flipped to Moroni in his scriptures and read a few passages about faith, miracles, and angels. Ben closed his scriptures. "I want you to know that I believe in miracles. In our ward, we're going through a terrible ordeal. As bad as it's been, it has taught us, me in particular, about the way the Lord works. We need to take Him at his word. He can and will work miracles, if we have faith and hope. What is hope? To me, it's happily and willingly being swallowed up in the will of the Father. When I was up on that mountain, frightened and frazzled, it wasn't until I completely submitted to the Lord that I felt at peace. It was a peace that washed over me like a warm shower. It was real. To me, that was a miracle, too. We must do everything we can and rely on the Lord to do the rest. For that to happen, we need to have faith and hope.

"In closing, I would like to quote Elder Neal A. Maxwell of the Quorum of the Twelve Apostles. It's something I've been trying to apply to my life: 'May we walk by faith, and, if necessary, even on our knees!'"

Ben's talk caused quite a commotion in the Helaman Sixth Ward. Members wondered if Ben knew something no one else did. Without coming out and saying it, ward members knew that Ben was saying there was still hope for Luke.

Some members were inspired. Others thought Bishop Kimball had gone a little overboard. They wondered if he was being overly optimistic or simply in denial. Nothing indicated that Luke would come back alive, if at all.

After the meeting, the stake president commended him. "I really felt the Spirit during your talk, Bishop Kimball," he said.

Bishop Law made it a point to track him down. "One of the best talks I've ever heard," he said. "This ward is in good hands."

22

Given his food intake, or lack thereof, Luke was withering away. For the first time since he was a foster child, he could actually see the outline of his ribs—one of which he was sure had been broken by King Noah. The good news was his flab had disappeared. He began thinking about starting his own new diet craze when—if—he returned home. He could call it the Sudanese Terrorist Diet—a bowl of rice a day. It certainly worked for him. Luke figured he had lost about twenty-five pounds. He decided he would never again complain about fasting, even to himself.

Scratching his chin, he felt his scraggly beard, which covered his face. He imagined he probably looked like an Old Testament prophet by now. He laughed to himself. *Hayley wouldn't even come near me with this rat's nest on my face*, Luke thought.

His leg had a bad scar, just as Dr. Allman had predicted, but at least he could move it. Luke was sure he had an infection of some sort. Not that his captors cared.

While he tried to sleep, his cell door opened and a man who he had never seen before left his bowl of rice on the ground. Luke feigned sleep as he watched the man walk away. The man inexplicably left the door ajar.

Finally, Luke thought, *they've gotten complacent, or careless.* He had waited months for that to happen.

Luke's heart began to beat fast. After all of this time, here was his chance to escape. He rose and cautiously approached the

117

door. Peering down the corridor, Luke didn't see a soul.

He didn't even know how to get out of the building he was in, let alone the terrorists' compound. And even if he somehow were able to get out of the compound, he had no idea where he was. Which way would he go? He had heard Khalid talk about wild animals—like lions—roaming about the countryside. Could he survive?

At that moment, none of that mattered. He ignored the consequences. All he could think of was his freedom. Luke believed that there had to be a way to get out. Maybe this was it.

After saying a silent prayer, Luke carefully opened the door, limped out of the cell, and moved quickly down the dark corridor. It was night time and all was quiet.

When he rounded the corner, he opened a door that led to a large, open area. There was a figure draped in an American flag, hung in effigy. In the distance, he saw rows of pictures of the Israeli and American flags he presumed were used for target practice.

He ran alongside a cement wall that surrounded the camp, hoping for an opening to escape. Unable to find one, he finally decided to climb over the wall. As he tried to scale the wall, he heard men shouting and creating a commotion.

Luke knew he didn't have much time. Weak but determined, he willed himself over the wall and fell hard onto the ground on the other side of the compound. He picked himself up off the ground and began running as fast as his injured leg would allow him. He wasn't able to sprint. It was more like a slow gallop. He had no idea where he was going; he just tried to get away from that compound.

Within minutes, he heard the sound of a jeep heading toward him. Knowing he wouldn't be able to outrun it, even with two healthy legs, Luke tried hiding behind a tree. The jeep's headlights were bright, so he held still. When the jeep turned a different way, Luke scrambled up the tree, hoping there wasn't some man-eating animal perched there already.

He was relieved to see the jeep going the opposite direction.

In the distance, he spotted an area filled with dense trees and brush. If he could only get there, where a jeep could not go, he might be able to escape.

Jumping down from the tree, Luke landed so hard he thought he might have sprained his ankle. But with all the adrenaline surging through his body, he barely noticed. He simply ran straight for the wooded area.

By that time, the men in the jeep had found Luke's trail of footprints, which led them to the tree. They did not find him there. With the aid of binoculars, they saw Luke, got back into the jeep, and gave chase.

The bright headlights shining on him ended his hopes for a successful escape. Still, he kept running as the men in the jeep gained on him. His life was over, he thought, but he wasn't going to give up without a fight.

The jeep caught up to him. A man jumped out and tackled Luke to the ground. Luke struggled with him and managed to push him off. As Luke stood again, ready to run, a second man knocked him down. One held his arms and sat on Luke's torso while the other held his legs. Another man pointed his gun at Luke's skull.

Khalid stepped out of the jeep and said something in Arabic to the man, who put the gun away.

"That was very stupid," Khalid said.

While the two men kept Luke pinned down, another jabbed a tranquilizer needle into Luke's leg to subdue him. Luke felt drowsy and felt himself slipping away.

They picked him up and dumped him in the jeep.

When he regained consciousness, Luke found himself back in his old cell. He lifted his head and saw Khalid and two men with guns standing outside his cell.

Khalid was not in a good mood.

"You thought you could make fools of us?" he shouted. "You are the fool. You will pay dearly for your mistake."

Then Khalid motioned to a large bearded man.

"King Noah," Luke joked. "Long time, no see."

The man lifted Luke up by the collar, rocked back and launched a ferocious punch at Luke's stomach. The force of the blow knocked Luke into the wall. Then King Noah grabbed a tuft of Luke's hair, slammed his head into the wall, and kicked him in the midsection, leaving Luke unconscious again.

23

HELAMAN, UTAH, USA

After what had seemed like a long, dark winter in Helaman, spring and summer arrived, right on schedule. It had been nearly five months since Luke had been kidnapped. Most people in the Helaman 6th Ward presumed that Luke was never coming back, considering so much time had passed. At one point, a report surfaced that Luke had been killed. The State Department said the CIA could not confirm or deny the report. Nobody seemed to know the truth.

With Luke's status in limbo, ward members continued to do everything they could for Hayley. Though she rarely left the house because of the bed rest edict imposed upon her, she had achieved a certain celebrity status around the country. She received hundreds of letters, postcards, and e-mails from every state, and a few foreign countries, from strangers expressing their sympathy. Some sent packages of cookies or rosary beads or silver crosses or Bibles. So much mail came to her that the post office in Helaman had to hire two more employees to handle the work load. It seems people were taken by the "Love You Forever" salutation and couples said they started saying it to each other every day.

Hayley hated being confined to a bed with nothing to do but read and watch TV. She longed to go up the canyon for a picnic or dancing or even bowling—anywhere but the hospital for a doctor's visit. The nurses would strap her to the ultrasound machine and monitor the baby's heartbeat and other vital signs.

Other than that, she stayed home. She rarely put on makeup and with her stomach protruding, she felt fat and ugly.

The household chores were left to the Relief Society sisters, who cleaned the house weekly and brought her two meals a day. Her visiting teachers would come by and give her a video to watch or a magazine to read.

The deacons, teachers, priests, elders, and high priests all pitched in to help, too. In the winter, they shoveled her walks and in the spring, they mowed the lawn. Her hometeachers stopped by on a weekly basis to check on her. Since she couldn't attend Church meetings, the Aaronic Priesthood holders brought her the sacrament on Sundays.

Primary children regularly drew pictures and wrote letters for Hayley.

The McMurray family, which traveled the world to sing their songs, held a benefit concert, with all proceeds going to a fund for Hayley and the baby. Brother Helton held a bake sale and a car wash to raise money for them.

"What's next?" Hayley joked when she was told about everything that was going on. "A telethon?"

She was appreciative of everyone's efforts, and she believed they were sincere in their desire to help, but she was also embarrassed to be the focus of so much attention and to be doted upon to such an exorbitant degree. She felt lazy because she didn't even have a Church calling. She felt like a burden on the entire ward.

But her mom reminded her that ward members were grieving, too, and they needed an outlet for their grief by serving.

"You've spent so much of your adult life serving others, in the hospital and on your mission," she explained. "Sometimes, you have to let others serve you. Besides, you've helped many people in this ward in the past. Now it's their turn to help you. At one time or another, we all need help."

Sister Woodard was always trying to encourage Hayley to eat. Doctors told her she needed to eat more, for the baby's sake, but she had trouble putting on enough weight. She found it difficult to eat anything.

Mostly, Hayley felt numb. She was holding out hope for Luke's safe return, but she also played the alternate scenario out in her mind, preparing herself for the worst. She believed in her heart that Luke was alive, but she realized that maybe it wasn't the Lord's will that he return home. In some ways, she thought, it would be easier if she knew he was dead. That way, at least she'd know he was safe, in the loving arms of the Lord, instead of being held captive by evil people. She was angry at those terrorists who had him. How could they do this to her husband, during what was supposed to be the happiest time of their lives?

Hayley and Luke had often talked about having children. Hayley knew Luke would be an outstanding father. Having grown up in a troubled home, Luke was determined to give his children all the love and stability he never had.

After they had married, Hayley and Luke frequently volunteered to babysit the Kimballs' children. Hayley watched carefully how Luke interacted with those kids. He was gentle, kind, and patient. He made them laugh. And she had heard all of the stories about how well Luke got along with Brooklyn before she had died.

Suddenly, Hayley was facing the real possibility that she would be a single mom. It scared her. She knew a few single mothers and always felt sorry for them. She didn't want people to feel sorry for her. She didn't want to be a lifelong charity case. Hayley grew up thinking that once she had a baby, her working days would be over and that her husband would provide for her and her family. It was dawning on her that perhaps those plans would have to change. Her parents could watch the baby while she worked, even though it wasn't the ideal situation. But what else could she do?

Hayley and Luke would talk about how their children were up in the spirit world, watching them. "I hope that about everything I did before my baptism will be edited out," Luke would say.

During the first few months of marriage, they bought a baby names book. Every week, they independently created a Top Ten list of favorite names, one for boys and one for girls. Then they'd get together and compare their lists.

Luke's favorites included Kirstie, Goldie, Shari, Mitzi, Jasmine, Monique, Miranda, Andrea, Lisa, and Kelsey for girls and Brody, Mitch, Toby, Zane, Rory, Flint, Hardy, Casey, Hogan, and Jake for boys.

"Those sound like names of soap opera characters," Hayley said.

She liked more traditional and Biblical names. Her girls' list was comprised of Sarah, Amy, Elizabeth, Emily, Marie, Eve, Miriam, Laura, Mary, and Susan. Her boys' list included Adam, Gordon, Jared, Abel, Ammon, Levi, Isaac, Aaron, Timothy, and Thomas.

"Pretty hip," Luke joked. "Our kids will get teased mercilessly at school."

"Looks like we're going to need a full nine months just to choose a name," Hayley said.

Due to disagreements over names and mounting frustration over Hayley's inability to get pregnant, those Top Ten lists were eventually buried in a drawer somewhere.

At least they agreed, for the most part, about how the kids would be raised. Luke and Hayley had already decided they would not spank their kids. Their children would grow up reading good books, memorizing scriptures, being involved in sports, and taking piano lessons. Hayley knew Luke wanted a son to take to ballgames. She also knew he'd be thrilled with a daughter. It didn't matter, as long as they had a child.

When members of the Relief Society would stop by her house, they would ask Hayley if she planned to find out if the baby was a boy or girl.

"No," she'd say. "Luke always said he would want us to wait to find out and I agree. We like surprises. So we'll wait."

Most of the ward members were convinced the baby was a boy. That way, he could be named Luke, Jr., in honor of his father.

The Relief Society asked Hayley if it would be okay to throw her a baby shower. Hayley agreed to it somewhat reluctantly. She fretted about the condition of the house, where everyone would sit, and how she would look.

The shower was held on a Saturday afternoon. Hayley's mom spent all Friday dusting, vacuuming, and cleaning. She also rearranged the furniture to accommodate everyone. Hayley did her hair and makeup and dressed in her best maternity clothes.

The living room was filled. The women played games, watched Hayley open gifts, and ate mint brownies and drank sparkling punch. Sister Helton made little baby booties for everyone filled with mints and peanuts. Hayley received enough packages of diapers to last until the baby was potty-trained. She received enough baby clothes—both for a boy and a girl—to outfit the entire Sixth Ward nursery.

Toward the end of the event, Hayley felt she should say something to express her gratitude. She stood up slowly.

"I feel overwhelmed by your love and generosity," she said. "Luke and I are really . . ."

Then she stopped, dropped her mint brownie on the floor and began crying. It had been a while since she had cried, and, suddenly, the tears came like a dam breaking. Her mom put her arm around her and escorted her to her bedroom.

The Relief Society sisters cleaned up the paper plates and wrapping paper and tidied up the house before leaving. Hayley was embarrassed to have lost control of her emotions in public like that again.

"When will this pain be over?" she asked her mother. "I can handle this discomfort and I think I can handle childbirth. But I don't know if I can go on much longer without Luke."

24

Hours after his latest beating from King Noah, Luke awoke. His head pounded as though someone was playing the bass drum on his cranium. He could barely open his eyes. Feeling groggy, he squinted and saw two bright figures with friendly faces appear across from him.

"Brooklyn?" Luke said. "Is that you again?"

"Yes. You look terrible, Luke."

"Yeah, well, that's what happens when you're being held captive by Islamic terrorists."

"You may be in prison, but at least you're not in spirit prison," Brooklyn said. "It could be worse. It's a good thing you got baptized."

Luke glanced at the girl next to her, the one with puppy-dog eyes, long eyelashes, and auburn hair.

"Esther, I presume?" Luke asked.

"Yes, you remembered her name," Brooklyn said excitedly. "She's very worried about you. But I told her everything will be okay."

"How do you know that? These people could kill me any minute."

"I know it looks bad, but you can't lose hope. You have so much to live for."

"I *had* so much to live for," Luke said. "I was married to Hayley and I was never happier. I guess I didn't realize that all that other stuff, worrying about not having a decent job and not

126

having money, didn't really matter. We had such big plans. We were going to have a big family. Now, we'll never have children."

"Luke, you shouldn't talk that way," Brooklyn said. "Heavenly Father has a plan for you. Trust in Him. You've got to have faith in that. There's a lot of people who have been praying for you. One thing I've learned is that sometimes things don't work out the way you think they will. But if we trust Heavenly Father, in the end, they will turn out better. He knows everything. He knows what's best. You have to believe that."

"I want to believe," Luke said.

"Just think of all of the times in the scriptures that Heavenly Father helped good people who were in prison," Brooklyn said. "My dad taught me all sorts of stories. Like the one about Shadrach, Meshach, and Abed-nego. A king with a long name I can't remember or say put them in a fiery furnace. They walked in the fire and did not get burned. And he saw another person, who the king said looked like the Son of God. Their hair wasn't even burned and they didn't even smell like smoke.

"And what about Daniel? He was thrown into a lion's den for praying to Heavenly Father. Some bad people put a big rock in front of the opening. Heavenly Father sent an angel to shut the mouths of the lions so they wouldn't hurt him. When the king came the next morning, he was glad Daniel was not hurt. Those guys who didn't like Daniel were thrown in the lion's den instead. No angels helped them, though.

"Remember Joseph? His dad made him a coat of many colors. His brothers were jealous so they threw him in a pit and sold him to some people who needed slaves. He ended up working for Potiphar. He was such a good slave that Potiphar told Joseph he could be in charge of his house. Potiphar's wife invited him to a sleepover, but Joseph got out of there so fast, his coat fell off. Even though he didn't do anything wrong, he was put in prison. He explained the dreams of two men who were there and the dreams came true, like Joseph said. Those men worked for the Pharaoh, the man in charge of the whole country. Then the Pharaoh started having weird dreams about seven scary cows that ate up seven good cows. Joseph interpreted those dreams, too. He got out of that prison and became the king."

"If only I could interpret dreams," Luke interrupted.

He looked over at Esther. She was just sitting there, smiling at him.

"And what about Abinadi?" Brooklyn continued. "He was preaching in the kingdom of the wicked King Noah. The guards took him as a prisoner, but Heavenly Father would not let anything happen to him until he was done with his mission. He made King Noah very mad because he spoke the truth. When he was done testifying to them, they burned him to death."

Brooklyn paused.

"Alma, who was one of King Noah's priests, believed Abinadi and he became a great missionary," she continued. "There's always a happy ending. Just like there will be for you. Somehow, some way, Heavenly Father will help you."

"Are you saying I'm going to make it out of here soon?"

"Only Heavenly Father knows," Brooklyn said. "You need to trust Him. You know, I'm kind of in prison, too, Luke."

"What do you mean?"

"I don't like not having a body. There are so many things I can't do. I'm separated from my family, too. I'm not allowed to talk to them like I can talk to you. I have to be patient. But we're both a lot better off than the people I see in the spirit prison. There are a lot of sad spirits there. I've taught them about Heavenly Father's plan and Jesus. Some don't want to listen. Those who repent get to come with us in paradise. That's why it made me so happy when you got baptized. I always knew you would."

Luke smiled.

"We have to go now," Brooklyn said. "Esther and I have other stuff we have to do."

"Like what?"

"I'm not allowed to say. Remember I told you about the rules?"

"Rules," Luke said. "Right."

Then they were gone.

Brooklyn and Esther seemed so real. Together, they shined like stars. They were beacons of hope, glowing in the darkness.

During his first few months of captivity, Luke prayed that he would be able to return home safely. After the latest visit from Brooklyn though, he learned that he needed to place his trust completely in the Lord's hands. He prayed that His will be done, no matter what, even if that meant dying.

25

During a ward function, Ben overheard more than a few of the ward members lamenting Luke's fate. They were talking about how after all this time, Luke had to be dead.

Ben, of course, believed otherwise.

He was becoming increasingly frustrated, though, by the lack of information coming from Senator Trammell, the State Department, and the CIA.

"Maybe I need to take matters into my own hands," Ben told Stacie one night as they were kneeling next to the bed, preparing for their nightly prayers.

"What do you mean?"

"I mean someone's got to do something. And it might as well be me. I'm responsible for sending Luke over there."

"Ben, I know you mean well, but what could you do?"

"I want to go to Washington, D.C., to meet with Senator Trammell and whoever else can help. There's got to be things going on they won't tell us about. I need to find out. I've left several messages for the Senator, on his answering machine and his e-mail. In the last one I told him he's lost my vote next November. When I try his office line, they always say he's at some meeting."

"Yeah, well, senators can get pretty busy."

"Too busy to help a citizen being held captive by terrorists?"

Ben's mind was made up and Stacie knew it.

"I'll have to use our Disneyland account to pay for this trip,"

Ben said. "I'll pay it back as soon as I can."

"Well, you're not going by yourself."

"If you come, who would watch all the kids?"

"No, I'm not going with you, for that very reason. Let's make a deal. I'll let you go if you can find someone to go with you."

"It's a deal," Ben said.

He spent the night going through the ward list in his head, trying to think of someone who might be able to leave his employment for a week or so at the drop of a hat.

Very few people in the ward fit that profile. Then he thought of Grit Woodard.

"Brother Woodard, this is Ben Kimball. I'm planning a little trip to Washington, D.C., to talk to Senator Trammell . . ."

Before Ben could invite him, Grit invited himself.

"I think that's a great idea. I'm coming with you."

Ben stopped by the home of Brother Gruber, the first counselor. As he stood on the porch, he was reminded of the time, years earlier, when he and Luke were paying him a hometeaching visit.

Ben had feared for his life that day, given Brother Gruber's gun collection and hostility toward the Church. It was a potentially explosive combination. That visit, though, was the beginning of Brother Gruber's turnaround. It also played a role in Luke's eventual conversion.

Ben couldn't believe how much had changed since then. He was the bishop, Luke was being held hostage in Africa, and Brother Gruber was a strong leader in the ward.

"Bishop," Brother Gruber said as he answered the door. "Come on in."

Instead of dead, stuffed animals on the walls as there had been during that first visit, there hung pictures of Christ and a copy of "The Family: A Proclamation To The World."

Instead of a can of beer, Brother Gruber held in his hand a can of grapefruit juice.

"Brother Gruber, I just came by to tell you I'm going to be going away for a few days."

"Business trip?"

"I'm going to Washington, D.C. to try to talk to Senator Trammell about Luke."

"Good for you," Brother Gruber said.

"I'm ready to try anything at this point."

"I really miss Luke," Brother Gruber said. "Our ward basketball team just isn't the same without him. Our whole ward isn't the same without him. Isn't it funny, though, how with him gone, the ward has never been closer?"

"Yeah."

"Without you and Luke, I don't know where I'd be today. That first time you two came over to visit me, I was angry. Back then, watching football on Sundays was my religion. I didn't stop to consider how much I was missing by not going to church. I was holding a grudge, not realizing the only person I was hurting was me. It took me a while to figure out that you don't go to church for the people, but you go for the Lord and for yourself. When you realize that, you look at the others who go to church in a different light. You look at them in the way the Lord looks at them. I just wanted to thank you again for teaching me that valuable lesson. Hopefully, I'll be able to thank Luke someday soon."

"I hope so, too."

Ben paid a visit to Sister Sterling, as he did every week.

"Any news about Luke?" she asked as she handed him a plate of cookies and a glass of milk.

"I'm sorry, Sister Sterling, there isn't."

"I'm still praying for him every day. He's such a nice young man. I feel so badly for poor Hayley, having to deal with a husband who is missing and expecting a baby. I know what it's like not having your husband around. How's Hayley holding up?"

"As well as can be expected," Ben replied. "She's really grateful for the ward's prayers and support."

"You know, I remember the first time I saw Luke and Hayley together. That was back when they were dating and Luke wasn't a member of the Church. I knew right away that they'd get married. You could just see it. Some couples just go so well together. They make a wonderful couple, just like you and Stacie."

"Thanks, Sister Sterling."

"Oh, before you go, I have something for you," she said, using her walker to get from the couch to the kitchen table. "I've had this for the longest time and I keep forgetting to give it to you. I have this check for $1,000 for Hayley. I want it to be anonymous. I'll leave it to your discretion, Bishop. I was looking on this tithing slip and all the different items to donate to—tithing, fast offering, perpetual education fund, missionary fund. I didn't know which one to choose."

"That's very kind of you, Sister Sterling. I know Luke and his family will appreciate it very much. I'll see that they get this."

"Make sure it's anonymous," she said.

"I will."

On the way home, Sister Fidrych flagged down Ben's car.

"Sorry, Bishop," she said. "I have a great idea for this year's July 24th sacrament meeting program. Would you have time Thursday night for a little presentation?"

"Actually," Ben said, "I'm going to be out of town that night. Feel free to contact Brother Gruber, though."

"Are you going on vacation?"

"No. I'm going to Washington, D.C., to find out more about Luke's status."

"Ooooohhhh!" Sister Fidrych said. "That sounds exciting!"

"Not really," Ben said. "Not very many people in the ward know I'm going. I don't want people to get their hopes up too high. It should be a quick trip. When I come home, I'll report to the ward what I found out. Until then, I'd appreciate it if you wouldn't mention this to anyone."

Ben should have known better. Telling Sister Fidrych to keep a secret was like telling a child to not play with toys.

26

Luke sat against the wall in his cell. He felt like he was inside an oven, basting like an Easter ham. He could tell summer had come. While he had frozen in the winter months, it was beginning to be unbearably hot.

As he was belting out "Come, Come ye Saints," Luke saw Khalid by the door, watching him. He was surprised to see him again after a lengthy absence.

"What is that you sing?"

"Church songs," Luke replied.

"Have you always been a religious man? Or are you proof of that saying—what is it?—that there is no such thing as an atheist in a foxhole?"

"No, I haven't always been a religious man. It wasn't until a couple of years ago that I started to believe in God."

"Is it your religion that tells you not to smoke or drink tea but instead sing those dreadful songs?"

"Yes. I used to think those songs were dreadful, too. Until recently."

"My religion also teaches that we shouldn't smoke," Khalid said, pulling out a cigarette. "But I have to. It calms my nerves. What are you, a Catholic?"

"No, I'm a member of The Church of Jesus Christ of Latter-day Saints."

"I have never heard of it."

"We're also known as Mormons."

"Never heard of them, either."

"We're working on that," Luke said.

"I walk by here day after day and see you singing those songs or on your knees, praying. You are wasting your time. You are a fool. Do you not know it is hopeless? Do you not know that you will die in this place? Your God cannot help you."

"My God will take care of me," Luke said resolutely. "Since you brought it up, when exactly will I die?"

"It is because of our mercy that you have been spared to this point."

"Can I ask you for a favor?"

"A favor?" Khalid said with a laugh.

"I'd really like to do some reading. It's been a long time. I've got a book in my bag. It has a handle and a zipper."

"What is this book?"

"Scriptures."

"The Bible?"

"Yes, and three other books, including one called the Book of Mormon."

"You'd be better off with the Quran."

"We believe the Book of Mormon to be the word of God."

"I suppose no harm could be done by letting you read," Khalid said. To Luke's surprise, Khalid left and returned with Luke's quadruple combination.

"What is this Book of Mormon?" Khalid asked.

Luke realized an opportunity to teach the gospel had just presented itself. He went through the entire Joseph Smith story and how he translated the Book of Mormon as Khalid listened intently. Luke felt more than a little strange having a spiritual conversation with a man who wanted to kill him. At the same time, he thought about how proud Hayley would be.

"I think you'd be surprised that the Mormon religion isn't all that different from the Muslim one," Luke said, drawing upon research he had done as a reporter.

"Nothing is like the Muslim faith, the one true religion of Allah," Khalid said.

"Really, we're not all that different."

"You are wrong."

"Look, we both believe in a higher power," Luke said. "Allah and God are different names for the same being."

Khalid looked pensive, then began reciting scripture.

"The Quran says, 'Allah is He Who created seven firmaments and of the earth a similar number. Through the midst of them descends His Command: that ye may know that Allah has power over all things, and that Allah comprehends all things in Knowledge.'"

Luke scrambled in the index until he found a certain scripture. "The Book of Mormon teaches the same thing, just in different wording," Luke said. "'Believe in God; believe that he is, and that he created all things, both in heaven and in earth; believe that he has all wisdom, and all power, both in heaven and in earth; believe that man doth not comprehend all the things which the Lord can comprehend.'"

"The Quran says 'Those who believe in Allah and work right-eousness, He will admit to Gardens beneath which rivers flow, to dwell therein forever: Allah has indeed granted for them a most excellent Provision.'"

"In the Book of Mormon, it says, 'And moreover, I would desire that ye should consider on the blessed and happy state of those that keep the commandments of God. For behold, they are blessed in all things, both temporal and spiritual; and if they hold out faithful to the end they are received into heaven, that thereby they may dwell with God in a state of never-ending happiness.'"

Khalid took the quadruple combination from Luke's hands for inspection. He leafed through the pages.

"When I'm dead, I hope you hold on to this and read it," Luke said. "Like I said, we believe this book to be the word of God."

Khalid continued to examine the book.

"You're well-versed in the Quran," Luke said.

"In my family, we memorized it. Every week, we gathered around the dinner table to learn of Allah's teachings."

"See? That's what I'm saying. We do that, too. We call it

family home evening. There are more similarities than differences between us."

"Do you believe the Quran to be the word of God?" Khalid challenged.

"We accept all truth, from whatever source. There are many good books out there, and the Quran is one of them."

"So this Joseph Smith is like your Mohammed."

"Yes, you could say that," Luke said. "Both men received inspiration and revelation on behalf of their peoples. Both are prophets. I believe Mohammed was a good, inspired man. We believe God loves all of His children, no matter where they live. God calls just men to teach them His truth. I've always respected and admired Muslims. Your people have made great contributions to philosophy, literature, history, medicine, and the arts."

"But you Mormons don't make pilgrimages to Mecca."

"Well, not to Mecca, but we know pilgrimages," Luke said. "The Mormons were persecuted and chased from their homes in the eastern United States and they fled to an unsettled territory in the West. Many died along the way. Those who survived arrived in a place now known as Utah. That's where I live. Also, we build beautiful buildings called temples for those who are obedient."

"We pray five times toward the holy city of Mecca each day," Khalid said.

"We have that many daily prayers, too," Luke said. "Even more on Sundays."

"We believe in almsgiving. We give one-fortieth of our income to the poor. Does your church help the poor?"

"Yes, we do the same thing. It's called fast offerings. Every month, we fast for twenty-four hours and take the money we didn't spend on food for those meals and give it to the poor. We also follow the law of tithing—we donate ten percent of our income to the Church."

"You Mormons fast, too? You have your own Ramadan?"

"Excuse my ignorance," Luke said, "but what exactly is Ramadan?"

"We abstain from food and drink from sunrise to sunset for

the whole month of Ramadan."

"We fast for twenty-four hours once a month. Sometimes, we do it for other occasions, like if someone needs a special blessing. See? We have a lot in common. We're not that different. I know that family is very important to Muslims, just as it is in my faith."

Luke looked into Khalid's eyes.

"We're brothers, you and me. Despite our many differences in the way we think and believe, we're brothers. We come from the same God. The same Heavenly Father."

As dark and dank as that cell was, Luke felt the Spirit of the Lord fill the space with light. Luke hoped that what he was saying would touch Khalid's heart somehow.

Khalid nervously shifted his feet and tried to avoid eye contact.

"I hate America and its policies toward Muslims," Khalid finally said. "But you seem like a good, just man. I must go now."

Khalid disappeared down the corridor.

Luke opened up the Book of Mormon and started reading where he had left off before he had been kidnapped. For the first time, he actually felt that there was a reason for him to be in that awful place.

27

Two days after Ben left the store in the capable hands of the assistant manager, and left the ward in the capable hands of Brother Gruber, he was on a plane, along with Brother Woodard, bound for the nation's capital. When he and Grit showed up at the senator's office, unannounced, the senator was shocked, to say the least.

"What are you doing here?" Senator Trammell asked. "You came all the way out here to see me?"

"You never returned any of my messages. I thought I'd have a better chance speaking to you in person."

"I'm sorry, gentlemen. I've been very busy."

The senator invited Ben and Grit into his office.

"We're doing everything we can for Luke. I am personally briefed by the CIA on this case every week. We're making progress. It's very unusual for these terrorists to keep a hostage for this long. I think that if we haven't heard anything, that's a good sign. Now, I don't want this part to get out because it could jeopardize some of our CIA operatives. But we think we know the general area where Luke is being held."

"Really?" Ben asked.

"Can't you send the military to go in and get him out of there?" Grit asked.

"There are special forces troops in the Middle East. Still, that would be a very dangerous move. We've got to be careful and deliberate in a situation like this."

139

"But Luke's life is at stake," Ben said. "Don't we need to act quickly?"

"We can't afford to endanger the lives of our troops unless we're sure about what we're doing. Ben, I'm sorry that this is taking so long. We have to keep being patient."

Ben was about out of patience, though he didn't say that to the senator. Instead, he and Grit thanked him for his time and went back to the cheap motel room where they were staying. They talked about how there had to be more that they could do. They started working on Plan B.

Ben called Stacie to check in and give her a report on how things went.

"So I guess that means you'll be coming home on the next flight back to Utah?"

"No, Stacie," he said. "Something's telling me I've got to go to Sudan."

"Ben, going to Washington, D.C. was crazy enough. But Sudan? Please tell me you're joking."

"I'm serious," Ben said. "Brother Woodard and I feel strongly that we should go over there."

"And do what? Look for Luke? That's like searching for a needle in a haystack. What are you two going to do that the government can't do?"

"Stacie, I don't know," Ben said calmly. "All I do know is, we need to do everything we can."

"You don't speak the language. You wouldn't even know who to talk to. I'm sure the Lord is doing everything He can."

"I believe that, too, but the Lord helps those who help themselves, right?"

"Ben, you have a responsibility to this ward. Not to mention your family."

"I've got to do this. Luke is a member of this ward. Wouldn't the Lord want me to leave the 'ninety and nine' and go find the one that's missing? And what about Hayley? I will never be able to live with myself if I don't do everything in my power to bring Luke home, or, at the least, find out what happened to him. She needs closure of some sort. I can at least give that to her. It's the equivalent of searching for my keys on the mountain."

"Ben, do you know how crazy that sounds? What do I tell people in the ward?"

"Tell them what I've told you. Brother Woodard and I have prayed about this. The Lord will protect us. If I were missing, wouldn't you want someone to try to find me? Think of Hayley. The least we can do is try to free him. If he's dead, at least we can bring some closure for her."

Stacie sighed. "What does the senator think of your plan?"

"He doesn't know about it. I did talk to Reverend Thurgood and he is setting up an appointment for us to meet with high-ranking leaders of the Sudanese government. Stacie, I don't know what's going to happen, but I feel so strongly that this is what we're supposed to do."

When Ben said that, Stacie was put somewhat at ease. She still wasn't crazy about the idea, but she trusted her husband's judgment.

For Ben and Grit, the big obstacle was getting to Sudan. The first step, Ben thought, was to get to Europe. Having served a mission in France years earlier, Ben had some friends in Paris, including a member of the Church who worked in the French government. He talked to the man, who said he would try to expedite the paperwork—visas and passports—so they could go to Sudan in a matter of days.

"What will we do once we get to France?" Grit asked Ben.

"I don't know, Brother Woodard. I'm just improvising as we go along."

Ben called Brother Gruber and told him he would be gone longer than he originally expected.

"You're going *where?*" That was Brother Gruber's immediate reaction. "I admire you for your courage and dedication, but don't be gone too long, or else Sister Fidrych might attempt some sort of coup and take over the ward."

Ben laughed. "You'll do fine," he said. "The ward will be fine. Let's just hope and pray that Luke will be, too."

Ben and Grit spent hours at the Dulles Airport in Washington, D.C., on standby, trying to find two open seats on the next plane to Paris. Grit was a little nervous since he had never left the continental United States in his life. But he was willing to do it, for his daughter, and his son-in-law.

28

Following his lengthy conversation about religion with Khalid, Luke was emboldened to delve further. He thought he should probably hold off on topics like baptisms for the dead and genealogy for some other time. Maybe, he thought, he could introduce the concept of eternal families.

Luke looked beyond himself, beyond his wife and his home back in Helaman, and put the Lord first.

Maybe this is why Brooklyn said my life has been preserved this long—to teach the gospel to Khalid. Maybe that's what Brooklyn meant when she said I had more work to do on this earth before I die.

He opened his scriptures and found some passages he could share with Khalid about God's love for His children.

When Khalid showed up, Luke smiled at him. Khalid wore a deadly serious look. He snatched Luke's quadruple combination so quickly that he ripped several pages. Before Luke could react, Khalid shouted at him while two armed men looked on.

"Your country has refused to comply with our demands. Therefore, you will die at sunrise tomorrow."

It was as if Khalid was a completely different person from the one Luke had talked to before.

"If that's the way it's going to be," Luke said meekly, "can I at least write my wife a goodbye letter or something?"

"You are in no position to make any requests!" Khalid yelled back. He spit on the ground, next to Luke's feet. "This is what your life is worth right now," Khalid said. "You are going to die.

Blessed be the name of Allah."

"C'mon," Luke said, "even you people can grant a dying man a final request."

Khalid grabbed Luke by the throat. "You will have no final request. You are no longer of use to us. And you will die a horrific death, the same as you Americans have subjected upon my Muslim brothers for so many decades. The hour for retribution is almost at hand."

With that, Khalid and his band of thugs were gone.

Luke had believed he'd made headway with Khalid. But he was wrong. He felt stupid and naïve. Obviously, either the man had been deceiving him earlier or else Luke had misread him. Then again, what did he expect trusting a terrorist? What made him really believe that this Islamic militant would be interested in the gospel of Jesus Christ?

Falling on his knees, Luke prayed that the fear would be removed from him. He prayed that he would be found worthy to return to the presence of the Lord. He prayed that the Lord would comfort Hayley and bless her with peace of mind, that they someday would be reunited and live together forever.

Luke imagined the litany of possible ways he could be executed. They could behead him, slit his throat, shoot him, drown him, burn him. He thought about what all of those people in the Bible and Book of Mormon must have felt in his situation.

Luke wished Brooklyn and Esther would come one last time. If they came, he thought, maybe Brooklyn could pass a message to Hayley. Luke waited and waited, but the only one to show up at his cell was Khalid, again. It was the last person he wanted to see.

"Come with us," he said to Luke as a guard placed handcuffs on him and pushed him out the door.

They took him to a room where a band of men wearing masks and armed with AK-47s stood against the back wall. The camera was rolling as they sat him in a chair.

"Not even your own country, the United States of America, cares if you live or die. How does it feel?"

Luke didn't say a word.

"Speak to the camera," Khalid demanded. "This is your chance for a final message. What do you wish to say?"

"Hayley," he said, "I love you forever."

"Beg for your life," Khalid ordered.

Apparently these Islamic militants were somewhat media savvy and they wanted good ratings. The more dramatic, the better.

But Luke refused to say anything else. He was determined to stare death in the face and not blink. He was determined to maintain his dignity to the bitter end. He refused to give them the pleasure of witnessing any tears, sadness, or fear.

One of the terrorists who stood behind him read a lengthy statement in Arabic. As he did, the others shouted, "Allah Akbar!"

Luke was escorted back to an open area of the compound. There, dozens of men, some dressed in combat fatigues, some dressed in turbans, stood around a giant bonfire like they were attending some sort of pep rally. They began clapping rhythmically and shouting in unison.

A man removed a wadded up American flag from a bag. Luke knew what was coming. The flag was tossed into the raging flames to the cheers of those who watched. They began chanting "Allah Akbar! Allah Akbar! Allah Akbar!" over and over again. "This is but a taste of what is to come," Khalid said to him. "Your execution will be shown throughout the Arab world and there will be rejoicing in the streets, for it will mark another victory over the American devils. Allah be praised."

"How you can justify this?" Luke asked. "How can you murder an innocent person in cold blood and claim to be doing it in the name of God? That's not the God I know."

While continuing to celebrate, the men then took Luke's belongings and tossed them into the blazing inferno. Gone were his computer, his wallet with pictures of Hayley, his scriptures.

The men took Luke back to his cell.

"Your final meal will be coming soon," Khalid said.

"Oh, great," Luke said. "Could I have a pepperoni pizza with Chicago-style crust, please?"

"Enjoy your last night here," Khalid replied smugly, closing the door behind him.

Facing imminent execution was unsettling, to say the least. Luke had hours left to live. On the other hand, at that point, he preferred to die than to spend any more time in that miserable cell.

29

For Ben, being in France again was bittersweet, of course. He had always dreamed of returning, though he'd wanted it to be under happier circumstances.

"My dad fought in World War II," Grit said as they sat on the Paris-bound plane. "He was involved in D-Day. He stormed the beaches of Normandy, you know."

"I didn't know that," Ben replied.

"Dad didn't talk about it much. I asked him what it was like when I interviewed him as part of an oral history. All he said was that war is terrible and he hoped future generations would never have to see what he saw and feel what he felt. He always said hatred is the most destructive force on Earth and that he witnessed it firsthand."

Their thoughts immediately turned to Luke again.

"Is it true that they eat a lot of snails over here?" Brother Woodard asked Ben as he put his seat in the locked and upright position.

"Yeah," Ben said. "It's true."

"You won't catch me eating any."

"Yeah, well, I don't plan to be here in France long enough to have the chance."

The jumbo passenger jet was making its final descent to Charles de Gaulle Airport and the pair couldn't wait to touch ground again. It had been a difficult flight. Just before take-off, Ben noticed Grit's face turn a shade of light green. Grit was hyperventilating and gripping the armrests with his fingers.

"Brother Woodard, are you okay?" Ben asked.

"No," he said, "but thanks for asking."

"You weren't nervous flying from Utah to Washington, D.C.," Ben said. "What's wrong?"

"I've never flown anywhere outside the United States," he replied, "and I've never flown over a large body of water. Like the Atlantic Ocean. I'll be all right."

But he wasn't all right.

"How about I trade you places?" Ben had asked. "Maybe I should be in the window seat."

"Good idea."

As the plane gained speed on the runway, Grit was wound up tighter than a spring. Ben found it somewhat amusing to see this big, tough cowboy be reduced to a pile of phobias in front of his eyes. Nobody ever dared mess with Grit Woodard, but he had finally met his match.

Then again, since Luke's kidnapping, Grit had revealed a much more sensitive side than anyone had ever seen of him.

Thankfully, he managed to fall asleep early into the flight. That is, until he was awakened abruptly as the 747 plummeted about 400 feet in midair. Passengers, including Grit, screamed loudly. Bolts of lightning flashed all around and sheets of rain pelted the plane. A flight attendant had spilled a scalding cup of coffee on a man sitting in front of Ben and Grit. The passengers scrambled to fasten their seat belts. Grit grabbed the airsickness bag in front of him and deposited his digested airplane meal into it.

The rest of the flight was relatively uneventful, but Ben and Grit knew the landing could be another adventure. So they engaged in small talk. Ben did what he could to keep Grit's mind off the landing.

"They call snails 'escargot,' you know," Ben said. "It's a gastro-nomic icon in France."

"Where do they get the snails?" Grit asked.

"People in the French countrysides go 'snailing.' They take a plastic bag and a walking stick and off they go. There are only certain times of the year you can do it."

"Like the deer hunt back home?"

"Something like that."

"How do you eat snails?"

"The one time I did it, it was on a dare from another missionary. I did it with my eyes closed. I think they put them in a large pot of cold water and slowly boil them. The snails go out of their shells on their own."

"The only French things I'll eat are French fries and French toast," Grit said, trying not to look out the window.

"Actually, those aren't really French."

"Really?"

"Yeah."

"French's mustard?"

"That's not French, either."

About then, the plane touched down. Everyone on board, including the flight attendants, erupted in applause.

Despite the dire circumstances surrounding their trip, and the horrible flight, Ben and Grit were upbeat. They considered arriving in Paris a major triumph. The way they saw it, they were a few thousand miles closer to Luke.

"Who's this guy we're going to see?" Grit asked as they retrieved their luggage.

"He's a man I taught on my mission here and he ended up getting baptized last year," Ben answered. "He sent me a photo of his baptism and everything. Anyway, he is an official in the French government. He said he could expedite our paperwork so we can get to Sudan as quickly as possible."

Ben and Grit arrived at the U.S. Embassy in Paris, where they had to wait for the bureaucratic red tape to be untangled. Officials at the embassy were working with Ben's friend to coordinate travel to Khartoum, Sudan, and a meeting with a Sudanese official. Ben had purchased two tickets and was hoping the visa and passport issues would be resolved quickly. He called Reverend Thurgood, who had set up a meeting at the Khartoum Airport with a member of the Sudanese government.

"I'll be praying for you," Reverend Thurgood said.

While Ben and Grit sat in the embassy lobby watching French television, Ben's ears perked up when he heard about a special report on an American being held hostage. An Arabic television network had obtained a tape of an American who had been held captive for more than eight months. Ben translated the words for Grit.

Suddenly, there was an image of Luke. He looked thin and pale. His hair was long and an unkempt beard covered his sunken face. "Hayley," Luke said softly, yet firmly, "I love you forever."

Behind him was the group of masked men holding guns. One held a large, shiny sword next to Luke's head.

"They say Luke will be killed in less than twenty-four hours," Ben told Grit grimly.

It was obvious this was no idle threat. Ben and Grit sat in silence for several minutes.

Neither of them dared say it, but they were both thinking that if nothing else, they could bring his body home from Sudan for a proper burial. Ben prayed that they would be able to recover Luke's body and he began thinking about funeral arrangements. He was hoping he'd survive his tenure as bishop without any funerals.

At least, Ben thought, Luke would be able to see Brooklyn again.

Ben recalled having all but promised ward members months earlier that if everyone exercised enough faith, Luke would come home. Had their collective faith not been strong enough? Or was this simply God's will? The situation, after all, had never looked more bleak.

Grit called home and learned that Hayley was in the hospital.

"The baby's heartbeat is faint," Sister Woodard said. "The doctors are very concerned. They're worried about Hayley, too."

"Does Hayley know about the latest news?"

"No."

"It's probably best to keep it that way. Her top priority right now should be delivering a healthy child."

Ben talked to Stacie, who told him that Brother Gruber had scheduled a special ward prayer.

"Everyone is fasting for Luke, for Hayley, and for the baby," Stacie said.

"We will be, too," Ben said.

His thoughts were simultaneously with ward members back in Helaman and with Luke. He couldn't imagine what Luke was going through. He didn't even know his wife was fighting to save their unborn child. Ben couldn't shake the disturbing image of Luke in that video.

Before long, Ben and Grit went to Charles de Gaulle Airport. Their flight to Khartoum would depart in five hours. For all they knew, Luke might be dead by then.

Grit and Luke hunkered down for a long wait in the terminal, wishing they were somewhere else, anywhere else. Amid all of the airport hustle and bustle, they were in their own little world of somber silence, reading their scriptures and keeping a constant prayer in their hearts.

Grit turned to Ben.

"Remember the first time I met Luke?" he asked.

Ben chuckled at the thought.

"I had never met anyone more cocky than him," Grit said. "I disliked him right off. I disliked the way he played basketball. When we were scrambling for the ball and my tooth was knocked out, I had never been more angry—at least in a church setting. All of those years branding cows and castrating bulls and nothing more than a scratch. One night of ward basketball with Luke and I lose a tooth."

"That was quite a night," Ben said.

"When he started dating Hayley after her mission, I thought I was going to go out of my mind. I kept wondering what she saw in him. He was arrogant, irreverent, and a non-member. Then he returned to New York and I was so happy. I thought we were rid of him forever. Next thing I know, Hayley goes to find him. I hoped it was just out of a spirit of missionary work, but deep down, I knew there was more to it than that. I'll admit that when he got baptized, I thought the worst. I thought he did it for Hayley. When Luke asked her to marry him, I told Hayley that I gave him two months of marriage for him to start slipping back to his old ways. I was convinced he would go inactive and revert to drinking and partying again."

"You told her that?" Ben asked.

"Yeah. I really believed that. But Hayley insisted it wouldn't be that way. I love her and I trust her. It turns out, she was right. Luke and I haven't always seen eye-to-eye. But you know what? He has been a good member of the Church and a very good husband. He's treated Hayley with respect and love. He's made her happy. What more could a father want for his daughter? It wasn't until he left that I realized that I love him like a son. I wish I could have had a chance to tell him that."

Grit returned to reading his scriptures. Ben bowed his head in silent prayer. Later that day, the picture of Luke with his masked captors would appear on the front page of every major newspaper in America and the world.

30

On his final night on Earth, Luke decided not to sleep. What was the point? He figured that without a body, sleep deprivation wouldn't be a factor in the spirit world. Besides, how could he sleep at a time like this?

Luke noticed himself trembling involuntarily. So he did the only thing he could do, the only thing he had done for the previous eight months—sing a hymn. One, in particular, he sung exultantly.

The Spirit of God like a fire is burning!
The latter-day glory begins to come forth.
The visions and blessings of old are returning
And angels are coming to visit the earth.
We'll sing and we'll shout with the armies of heaven,
Hosanna, hosanna to God and the Lamb!
Let glory to them in the highest be given
Henceforth and forever, Amen and amen!

Luke didn't see him, but Khalid stood outside the cell for a few minutes, listening to the hymn before going to set up for the upcoming execution.

When Luke's voice became too hoarse to sing, he knelt to pray some more. He asked Heavenly Father to be with Hayley. He prayed that one day she would be able to have children.

"I know this is all part of Thy plan," he said.

Luke wondered what dying would be like. He wished he

would have asked Brooklyn that question, though he knew she probably would have told him that was against the rules.

He imagined being welcomed into the arms of the Savior. He decided that's the mental image that he would keep in his mind during the last few hours of his life.

While he was praying, Luke was interrupted by Khalid, who entered the cell alone, carrying a semiautomatic rifle.

"That was a quick night," Luke said. "Time flies when you're about to be murdered."

Khalid pulled Luke's head back by his hair and whispered, "Keep your mouth shut." Then he placed a hood on Luke's head and ordered him out of the cell.

Luke was too weak, too tired, and too scared to talk back anymore.

They walked a long distance, as far as Luke could tell, with the gun in his back. He wondered if these guys had a special execution room for the occasion. Luke noticed it was quiet and he could tell he was outside. Strange thing was, if it were nearly sunrise, why were there no birds chirping? Khalid said nothing and Luke was surprised to hear no noises around him.

Suddenly, he felt Khalid remove the gun from his back and heard a door open slowly. "Walk forward," Khalid ordered.

Luke did as he was told. The door shut behind him.

Khalid removed the hood quickly. Luke recognized the area in front of him from the time he had unsuccessfully tried to escape.

Confused, Luke looked at Khalid for an explanation. Were they going to take him to another location for his execution? Before Luke could ask, Khalid stretched out his arm, pointed his finger, and said matter-of-factly, "If you go northwest—that way—and move quickly, you can reach the nearest town in a couple of days, if wild animals don't get to you first. But you must hurry."

Then Khalid handed Luke a pair of boots to put on his bare feet. "These should fit you."

"Is this some sort of trick?" Luke asked.

"No trick."

"I don't understand. You're letting me go? I'm free? But what about all those friends of yours who are foaming at the mouth to watch me die?"

"You must leave now."

Luke quickly slipped his feet into the boots and tied the laces. "Why are you doing this?"

"I had a strange dream tonight. Two young girls—they looked like American girls—came to me in this dream. They said they were sent from Allah and I must free you. After that, I could not sleep. I could not rest unless I did this thing. So I got out of bed and got the key to your cell. If they find out what I have done, I will be killed. If you are recaptured, which is a strong possibility, I will deny any knowledge of this."

"Your secret's safe with me. Thank you so much for doing this," Luke said, shaking Khalid's hand for the first time.

"Do not thank me," Khalid said. "You still may not survive."

Luke looked his captor in the eyes one last time.

"Thank you, my brother," he said. Then he turned and began running as fast as he could.

"Goodbye, my brother," Khalid said to himself as he watched Luke running away. "May Allah watch over you."

Luke tried not to think about the wild animals that roamed the land and he tried not to wonder how long it would be before the terrorists discovered he was missing and came looking for him. All he knew was that if he were recaptured, he would not go back there alive. Luke thanked the Lord for sparing his life. He thanked the Lord for softening Khalid's heart. He thanked the Lord for Brooklyn and Esther.

Because of the adrenaline coursing through his body, Luke ignored the pain in his leg and the fact that he was about out of breath. Like the pioneers who pushed those handcarts, he knew he had to keep going. Luke was glad to be wearing boots. Without them, he wouldn't have been able to get far on the harsh terrain.

All of the time he'd spent running in place in that cramped cell was paying off, Luke thought. Still, he had no idea if he was going in the right direction. He just wanted to be as far away from those terrorists as possible.

As dawn broke in the distance, Luke heard the sound of a vehicle speeding toward him. He knew it was not a good sign. Luke continued running, willing his body to keep going beyond its strength and power. He turned and saw a van gaining on him. His left foot landed in a small hole and he tripped. As he tried to stand up, the van stopped. Three men dressed in long robes and turbans stepped out, holding semiautomatic weapons. Luke could not see their faces.

He managed to get to his feet. "I am not going back there!" Luke yelled at them. "You're not going to take me alive! You're going to have to kill me!"

Then he heard a man's voice announce, in plain English, "Sir, identify yourself! Please tell us your name and tell us who you are."

Once again, Luke was confused.

"My name is Luke Manning," he said. "Who are you?"

The man removed the turban from his head, put down his gun, and smiled. "It's okay, Mr. Manning," he said. "We represent the United States Marines."

"You're really the good guys?" Luke asked.

"Yes, sir. We're going to get you home."

"You guys wouldn't happen to be the Three Nephites, would you?"

"Huh?" they replied in unison.

"Sir, we're members of the special ops forces. We've come to take you back to the United States of America."

"You're Army Rangers," Luke said in wide-eyed bewilderment, as if he were a six-year-old kid.

"Yes, sir."

"You are my new best friends."

Luke boarded the van with the three Rangers and they quickly left. The trio introduced themselves to Luke.

"You guys always dress like this?" Luke asked.

"No sir," said Sgt. Parker from Topeka, Kansas. "Only when we're trying to find an American in trouble. We've been out here for weeks, talking to villagers, trying to get information about the terrorist camp we believed you were being held in. We try to blend in as best we can."

"You looked pretty convincing to me," Luke said.

He asked them what was going on at home in the world of politics and sports. "Are the Mets in first place?" he asked.

"No clue," said Sgt. Wisemueller from Macon, Georgia. "We've been deployed in the Middle East for more than 18 months now."

"What are you guys doing in Sudan?"

Sgt. Wisemueller smiled. "We came looking for you."

One of the Army Rangers, Sgt. Bellini from Oceanside, California, was on a satellite phone, talking to an Apache helicopter pilot.

After driving a couple of miles, the Rangers ditched the van. The Apache roared overhead, then landed in the desert, kicking up dust for hundreds of yards. The pilot, who was wearing a jumpsuit featuring a small American flag patch, shook Luke's hand vigorously.

"Congratulations," he said. "I'll bet they'll planning your homecoming parade soon."

"Can you guys or someone let my wife know I'm okay?" Luke asked.

"We're working on that," Sgt. Wisemueller said.

As the Apache rose into the sky, Sgt. Bellini told Luke how surprised they were to find him.

"What kept you going all those months?" he asked Luke.

"Saying prayers," Luke said, "and singing church hymns."

"How did you escape?"

"It was a miracle," Luke said. "Nothing but a miracle."

"Let's get you home," Sgt. Wisemueller said.

"I like the sound of that plan," Luke said.

His harrowing eight-month ordeal was almost over. He still needed to get home.

31

Luke sat in the hospital bed with a cup of ice water in one hand and a Snickers bar in the other. He tried to walk around, but with the catheter strapped to his body and an IV stuck in his arm, he was tethered to his hospital bed. It was surreal to be in a bed, wearing clean clothes, and eating something other than rice.

He reached over and searched for a phone. There wasn't one. *What kind of a hospital doesn't have a phone?* he thought.

Luke heard a knock on the door of his room.

"Come in," he said.

A nurse poked her head in. "Oh, good," she said. "You're awake. Anything else I can get for you?" she asked.

"Yeah," Luke said. "When can I call my wife?"

"A military chaplain is on his way. When he arrives, you'll be able to talk to her. We're working on that as fast as we can."

"Do you think she knows I'm free?" he asked.

The nurse laughed. "Mr. Manning, I think everybody in the world knows you're free. It's big news." She walked over to the window. "Right down there are dozens of cameras and reporters. When you leave, they will be trying to get pictures of you."

"Great," Luke said. "I go from being held by terrorists to being stalked by the paparazzi."

"Tell me," the nurse said, "how did you escape those horrible people?"

Luke smiled. "It was a miracle," he said. "That's all I can say."

"I understand if you don't want to talk about any of that

right now," the nurse said as she left. "You keep resting."

But Luke was tired of resting. All he wanted to do was talk to Hayley. He wondered where she could be, what she was doing.

Luke tried to retrace the previous hours. The Apache helicopter carried Luke and the Army Rangers from Sudan to Prince Sultan Air Base in Al Kharj, Saudi Arabia, south of Riyadh. When they were preparing to land in what looked like a giant parking lot in the desert, Luke couldn't help but think of Khalid. He wondered if his captors had found out what he had done. If so, what would happen to Khalid? He no longer thought of him as an enemy, but as a friend, a brother. Luke hoped he would get out of that terrorist network.

While at the base, Luke tried to call Hayley at home. There was no answer. Luke called Hayley's parents. No answer there, either. The Kimballs' line was busy. By then, it was time to board a military jet for Landstuhl Regional Medical Center, the largest American hospital outside the United States.

"We'll keep trying to get a hold of your wife," a colonel at the base promised Luke.

Once Luke arrived at the hospital, he showered and shaved for the first time in months. He stroked his clean-shaven face. He had gotten used to the scruffy beard.

Nurses drew Luke's blood and a team of doctors examined him. He felt like a Guinea pig. They told him they couldn't believe he hadn't died from that knife wound in his leg, let alone from an infection.

"Believe it or not, a very good doctor treated me there," Luke explained.

The doctor told Luke he would begin the repatriation process. A team of mental health experts were eager to talk to him.

"Before we release you, we want to ensure that you're okay," the doctor said.

"How long will that take?" Luke asked. "Believe me, now that I'm out of that cell, I'm fine. Just because I've been locked up in a cell by a bunch of Muslim radicals for three-quarters of a year doesn't mean I'm crazy or anything."

"We know that," the doctor said. "But you've been subjected to a horrific experience. You may suffer from post-traumatic stress disorder. We just want to help you assimilate back to society in an orderly and timely manner."

"When can I talk to my wife?" Luke asked.

"We're working on that," the doctor answered.

"I just want to talk to my wife as soon as possible."

"As soon as we contact her, we'll let you know."

Luke's eyelids snapped shut and he slept for hours. When he awoke, all he wanted was a phone to call Hayley. He just wanted to go home.

There was another knock on the door.

"Mr. Manning," the nurse said, "you have some visitors."

"I hope it's someone with a phone," Luke muttered.

Ben and Grit walked into his room. They were beaming.

Luke smiled back. Ben and Grit greeted Luke with a hug. It was the first time Luke remembered Grit being affectionate with him.

"How did you get here so fast?" Luke asked.

"We were in the neighborhood," Ben answered. "We happened to be in Paris and when we heard the news of your escape, and that you were in Germany, we got on a train that brought us here."

"What were you doing in Paris?"

"Trying to get a flight to Sudan to find you."

Luke looked at Grit. "*You* were coming to find me?"

"We weren't going there for a vacation," Ben said.

"Where's Hayley?" Luke asked.

"She's home," Grit answered.

"She's not with you?" Luke asked.

"You haven't talked to her yet?"

"No," Luke said.

"You've got to talk to her right away. I'm going to get you a phone right now," Grit said. "I'll be right back."

He returned with a hospital chaplain, the hospital public relations director, and a phone.

"We've tracked down your wife," the chaplain said. "She's on the line right now." The chaplain hooked up the phone and asked the hospital operator to transfer the call to Luke's room.

Luke's heart was racing as he grabbed the phone. Ben, Grit, the chaplain, and the PR director left the room.

"Hello?" Luke said, hearing a slight echo.

There was long-distance crying on the other end of the line.

"Hayley, it's me. This is like one of those cheesy MCI commercials."

"Is it true?" she asked. "I didn't want to believe it until I heard your voice. Are you really okay?"

"Yeah, aside from some bumps and bruises. Ben and your dad are here with me. We'll be home as soon as we can. The doctors want me to rest up a bit."

"Enjoy the rest while you can," Hayley said, sniffling. "You'll need all your rest for the diaper changes and 3 a.m. feedings."

Luke sat up so fast in his bed that he nearly snapped his spine. "I'm confused," he said. "What are you saying?"

"What I'm saying is," Hayley said, crying, "you're going to be a father any day now."

"I'm going to be a dad?" He paused and did some quick math in his head. "I *am* the father, right?"

Hayley laughed until she started to cry again. "I'm glad you still have your sense of humor."

"You mean all this time, you've been pregnant, and I had no clue?"

"That's right. You missed the morning sickness, the doctor's visits, the ultrasounds, the bed rest. Hopefully you'll be here for the big moment."

"Nothing's going to stop me from being there. Now, you've waited this long, can you wait a couple more days? I don't want to miss that for the world."

"Well, you'd better hurry. This baby's due date is not up to me. Luke, there have been a few complications with the pregnancy, so the doctors are really monitoring me closely . . ."

"What kind of complications?"

"I've just been under a bit of stress these past eight months. Go figure. In fact, I'm calling you from the hospital right now. I'm having contractions every eleven minutes."

"As much as I'd like to be there to see the baby be born, you do what the doctors tell you so you can take care of yourself and the baby. I'll be there as soon as I can. Okay?"

"Okay."

"You don't know if it is a boy or girl, do you?"

"Of course not. We decided we wouldn't find out and I haven't. Though everyone in the ward begged me to."

They bounced some boy and girl names off of each other.

"If it's a boy," Luke said, "how about Khalid?"

"What?" Hayley replied.

"I'll explain it to you later."

"Do you know how great it is to hear the sound of your voice?" Hayley asked.

"I was just thinking the same thing. Look, I'm going to work on getting out of here. Hayley, I love you forever."

Hayley let out a loud yelp.

"Hayley?" Luke asked.

"I'm okay," she said. "Just another contraction. I love you forever."

Luke hung up the phone and immediately began removing the monitors from his body. His ankle was sore and tender, but he had to get home. Wearing nothing but a hospital gown, he opened the door of his room to find two armed American military personnel standing sentry outside.

"Can we help you, sir?" one of them said.

"Are you guys making sure I stay in my room?" Luke asked.

"No, sir. We're here to make sure you get home."

"Well, I'm ready. Let's go."

The nurse showed up and quickly ushered him back to his bed.

"Mr. Manning," she said, "you really shouldn't be up and moving yet."

"My wife is going to have a baby any minute now and I need to go home."

"I know," the nurse said. "It's all over the news. We're doing everything we can."

Ben and Grit returned to the room.

"Congratulations, Dad," Ben said, embracing Luke again.

"You're going to be a great father," Grit said.

Luke was beginning to wonder if his real father-in-law had been abducted by aliens.

The doctors wanted to do more tests on Luke, then transfer him to Walter Reed Hospital in Washington, D.C. But Ben and Brother Woodard spoke to Senator Trammell, who flexed his political muscle on Luke's behalf. He convinced the doctors to release Luke so he could be reunited with Hayley as soon as possible.

"We've got great news," Ben told Luke. "The doctors said they're going to let you go in a couple of hours. Usually, in a case like this one, the military flies the spouse here for a reunion at the hospital. But given the unusual circumstances, they're not doing that this time. They're going to fly us to Washington, D.C., where we'll change planes, and then go to Salt Lake City."

While in the hospital room, Luke shared with Ben a little bit about his travails. He told him about Khalid and how he actually taught him a little about the gospel.

"I guess that would make you the first unofficial Mormon missionary in Sudan," Ben said.

"This might sound weird to you, and I'll explain it all in detail to you sometime, but I want you to know that Brooklyn helped me while I was there."

Ben's eyes filled with tears.

"You know, that doesn't sound weird at all," he said. "I can't wait to hear about it."

After a pause, Ben said, "You know, just because you were gone for almost nine months, you're not off the hook. You're still speaking in sacrament meeting in a couple of weeks, okay?"

"Okay, Bishop," Luke said, smiling.

Before Luke was allowed to leave, some mental health professionals asked him questions and gave him an abbreviated repatriation course. One of the steps in the process, Luke was told, was writing down his experiences. Luke assured them that he would, and in great detail.

"That's the best therapy we can recommend," they said to Luke.

When the questioning ended, Luke dressed in some clothes Ben and Grit had purchased for him. Besides his wedding ring, all of the possessions he had taken to Sudan were gone. There was nothing to pack.

Before leaving, Luke was pulled aside by the hospital public relations director. "There are a lot of reporters and TV cameras out there," he said. "Everyone back home has been following this story. The media wants you to make a comment. Are you up to it?"

"Yeah," Luke said, "but it's going to be short."

Luke walked out of the hospital, flanked by Grit and Ben and military personnel. They were nearly blinded by the flashes of the cameras. He stood at a podium, which was filled with microphones. Ben was glad he wasn't in the spotlight anymore. All the national news networks carried Luke's comments live.

"A couple of days ago, I thought I would never see my wife again. Soon, I'm going to be reunited with my wife and I'm going to meet our new baby. I can't think of a better homecoming gift than that. It's a miracle and an answer to many, many prayers. I want to thank everyone who prayed for me. I feel so fortunate to be alive. I know the odds were stacked against me, so being free again is like winning the lottery. I can't wait to go home to Helaman, Utah, watch a Mets game on television, and eat a nice, juicy steak. I want to tell my wife, Hayley, that I love you forever and I'll be home as quick as I can. Thank you."

As the reporters shouted out questions, Luke and his entourage stepped into a military-owned SUV and headed for the Frankfurt airport.

32

HELAMAN, UTAH, USA

By the time Luke, Ben, and Grit arrived at Salt Lake International Airport, they were exhausted and thrilled at the same time. Ben immediately called Stacie for an update on Hayley's condition.

"You'd better hurry," Stacie said. "Her water broke this morning and the doctors have done everything they can to delay the birth. But this baby seems determined to come today. Hayley's been in labor for the past six hours."

As previously arranged, they got into a police car for an escorted trip, at 75 miles-per-hour, south down I-15 to Utah Valley Regional Medical Center in Provo. Ben kept calling Stacie for updates. Luke was sick with nerves.

"I don't know what to do," he said. "I've never even been to a Lamaze class."

Grit laughed. "Take it from me," he said. "The secret is to let the woman and the doctors do all of the work."

More cameras and reporters were gathered at the hospital, waiting for Luke's arrival. "It's going to be a media circus," said the police officer who was driving the car.

"Ben," Luke said as they passed a crowd of people in front of the hospital, "what's up with all these T-shirts that say 'I love you forever'?"

"It's a catchphrase that's been sweeping the country since you've been gone," Ben answered.

Police officers had to push the media back when the car pulled up to the front door. Luke was met by a doctor, who rushed him to labor and delivery.

"Your wife is at a nine and almost fully effaced," he said.

"What does that mean? Is that good or bad?" Luke asked.

"It means you better get into these scrubs as fast as you can."

Luke put on the gown, the gloves, and the hat. The doctor practically dragged him to the delivery room.

The first thing Luke saw when he walked into the room was Hayley's face. She was reclined on a bed, grimacing in pain, and when she saw Luke she tried to smile, but she was too busy breathing. Luke immediately grabbed her hand and kissed her cheek. She clung to his hand with all of her strength.

"Mr. Manning," one of them said, "you've got impeccable timing. We can see the top of the baby's head."

Luke looked down.

"The baby has hair," Luke told Hayley, on the verge of hyper-ventilating. "Quite a bit of it, actually."

Moments later, the doctors pulled out a tiny, purplish body covered in liquid and blood. Luke looked for something that would identify the gender.

"It's a . . . a . . . girl, right?" Luke asked the doctor.

"Yep. A beautiful baby girl. Congratulations to both of you."

"Hayley!" Luke exclaimed. "It's a girl!"

"Mr. Manning, would you like to cut the cord?" a doctor asked.

"You'll really let me do that?" Luke replied. "I thought they only did that in the movies."

"Well," the doctor said, "considering these circumstances, this is like a movie."

Luke took the scissors and snipped the cord.

While the doctors placed the baby in a blanket and began performing a battery of tests, Luke bent down and gently kissed Hayley again. She embraced him and cried. "I can't believe you're here," she said.

"I can't believe we're parents," Luke said. Just then, the little infant let out a scream, and then started crying.

"Your baby looks—and sounds—just fine," a nurse said, placing the baby in Hayley's arms. "We're going to take her down to the nursery to be weighed and measured. Then we'll give her a bath."

"Go with her," Hayley said to Luke. "Take the video camera so I can see her first bath."

The moment rivaled his wedding day. Every day while being held in that cell in Sudan, he had dreamed of returning home, and this exceeded every expectation. He was reunited with his wife and met his daughter all in the span of a few minutes. As he carried the precious baby in his arms, he studied her little face. He couldn't have asked for a better homecoming gift. She looked so familiar to him, as if he had known her for years. Luke was amazed how quickly the bonds of fatherhood were created. Already he was thinking about the guys that would date her. Then he thought of Grit and, for the first time, could empathize with him.

Then, in an instant, the name of his daughter came to him. He couldn't wait to tell Hayley.

"Mr. Manning," said the nurse, who was crying, "I just want you to know how happy we are that you are home safely. We've all been praying for you."

"Thanks," Luke said. "All of our prayers were answered."

As the nurses made a fuss over the baby, cooing about how cute she was, they weighed her—she was six pounds, three ounces—and bathed her. Luke caught it all on tape.

He heard a tapping on the nursery window. Luke looked away from his camera and saw Ben, Stacie, and Hayley's parents standing there, dying to see and hold the baby.

The nurses dressed the baby in a diaper and an undershirt, then wrapped her up tightly. They placed a pink beanie on her head.

"Mr. Manning, do you know the name of the baby yet?" a nurse asked. "We would like to put it on her chart."

"I've got to discuss it with my wife first. We haven't really had a normal conversation in, oh, about nine months."

Luke proudly carried the baby to the recovery room, where Hayley and her parents were anxiously waiting. Sitting on the table next to her bed were a dozen red roses that Luke had told Ben to pick up for her. Luke looked at Hayley, lying in her bed, without makeup, without her hair done, completely worn out. She had never looked more beautiful to him than at that moment.

"No offense," Grit said to Luke, "but I think she looks a lot like Hayley."

"Lucky girl," Luke replied.

"So, what is going to be the name of our beautiful grand-daughter?" Sister Woodard asked.

Hayley and Luke looked at each other. "We'll get back to you on that," Hayley said.

33

The doctors and nurses were still concerned about Luke's condition and they offered to get him a bed downstairs. But Luke insisted on staying in Hayley's room, with her and the baby.

When Luke woke up the next morning after spending the night sleeping in a chair, he suffered from a badly kinked neck. He could barely move it from side to side.

"Nine months sleeping on a cold, hard floor and I never had any neck problems," Luke said with a laugh.

For the next twenty-four hours, Luke spent every moment with Hayley and the baby. Meanwhile, the media frenzy continued.

Reporters begged for photos of the new family. That meant Ben was back to being the family spokesman again. He provided a picture of Hayley, Luke, and the baby in the hospital room to the press and then asked them for some privacy. "They just need time together," he said.

Naturally, the press was clamoring to know the story about how he escaped the terrorists after the death sentence had been pronounced upon him. But Luke wanted to tell his unbelievable story in his own way. The No. 1 rule of journalism, after all, is never let the competition scoop you.

After most of the media people left, Ben visited the Mannings and tendered his resignation. "As of right now," he said with a laugh, "I'm officially retired as your spokesman."

"C'mon, you might have a real future in this," Luke joked.

"No," Hayley said. "We don't need any more experiences like this."

Throughout the day, gifts from strangers were delivered to the room. Many people from around the country had written notes or faxed letters or sent e-mails congratulating Luke on his return and the birth of his daughter. The nurses in the maternity ward chipped in and bought the family five or six pink and yellow outfits for the baby.

That night, Luke and Hayley watched the ten o'clock news from her hospital room and saw the report about the homecoming.

Hayley reached out and took Luke's hand. "I still can't believe you're home," she said. She caressed his bruised face. Then she rubbed his stomach. "You're so skinny," she said. "We're going to have to fatten you up."

"I can't wait," Luke said.

He carefully picked up the sleeping baby and cuddled with her. "We should probably figure out what her name's going to be," Luke said.

"Okay," Hayley said. "If you look inside the bottom of my suitcase, you'll find those Top Ten lists we did a long time ago."

They went through their lists of girl names. None of the names really stood out. Then Luke pitched the name that had come to him earlier and they discussed it at length.

The next day, hospital personnel released Hayley and the baby. They sneaked them through a side door, away from the few media members that remained. Hayley already had the car seat strapped in.

"This was a gift from the Relief Society," Hayley told Luke.

They returned home to find dozens of American flags lining the front yard and dozens of pink balloons tied to the porch. Someone had placed signs in the front yard. One exclaimed, "It's a girl!" and the other said, "It's a Luke!"

When he opened the door to his house, with his new daughter in one arm and Hayley on the other, Luke felt like the happiest man in the world. It didn't matter that his house was aging or that the bathroom sink had a leak or that the ceiling had begun to crack. He was home, and it was a beautiful sight.

The old house was filled with baby items, thanks to the

generosity of so many people, including hundreds of strangers. Luke's office was filled with boxes of diapers and baby wipes.

"There wasn't enough room in the nursery," Hayley explained.

There were stacks of letters from people all over the world that needed to be read and answered.

Finally, they were a family again. Luke was determined never, ever to take anything for granted again.

July 24—Pioneer Day—rolled around a couple of days later. Organizers of the annual Helaman parade asked Luke, his wife, and their daughter to be the Grand Marshals. It would be their first public appearance together. So, a parade that was usually just ignored by everyone outside of Helaman suddenly became national news.

In Helaman, the parade was the biggest thing to hit Main Street every year. Of course, Main Street wasn't very long, so neither was the parade. It always included Boy Scouts carrying American flags, a few farmers riding their horses or tractors, Primary kids singing on a float, politicians throwing stale candy to the kids, and business owners promoting their goods or services by tying in a Pioneer theme. The Munchaks had an elaborate float that Brother Munchak drove every year featuring a giant seagull made of flowers and crepe paper swooping down to eat a huge cricket.

"Don't expect seagulls to be the solution to your food storage problem," a sign on the side of the float read. "Be prepared. www.munchakmunchies.com."

This year was no different. Except that Senator Trammell flew out from Washington, D.C. to be involved in the festivities. He spoke to the crowd and to the media before the parade, knowing the appearance and photo ops would probably be worth a few more votes come re-election time.

"Just as the pioneers did more than 150 years ago, Luke endured hardships of every kind," Senator Trammell said. "Now, he's back home in this special country, in this special town of Helaman, Utah."

The crowd went wild.

Afterward, Ben thanked the senator for all of his hard work. When Ben had found out that Army Rangers had rescued Luke after his escape, he apologized for doubting the Senator's efforts.

A group of men dressed in kilts played "Come, Come Ye Saints" on their bagpipes. Following behind them was Luke, Hayley, and the baby, riding in the back of a red convertible. They were, of course, the highlight of the parade since everyone wanted to see them together. As they passed by, the crowd jumped to its feet, applauded, and took pictures.

Hayley waved like a homecoming queen and Luke bit his cheek so he wouldn't start crying. The street was lined with teary-eyed, cheering spectators.

Before returning home with his family, Luke met Senator Trammell and thanked him for all of his work behind the scenes. He also greeted ward members and shook hands with well-wishers.

When it was all over and the last of the horse manure had been cleaned up, the Mannings hurried home to feed the baby. When she was done eating, Luke burped her, then put her in the bassinet. Hayley had begun to sing a lullaby to her when the phone rang.

"It's probably my mom," she said. "I'll get it."

Moments later, Hayley returned. "Luke," she said, "it's for you."

They were receiving a lot of phone calls. Luke was in high demand from members of the Church who wanted him to speak.

"Hello," Luke said.

"Luke Manning?"

"Yes."

"Jack Kilborn here."

At first, Luke thought it was Ben playing a practical joke. But nobody could imitate Kilborn's gravelly voice.

"Jack," Luke said. "This sure is a blast from the past. I never thought I'd be hearing from you again in my lifetime."

"I know. But I wanted to congratulate you on returning home safely."

"Is this *the* Jack Kilborn, the ruthless publisher?"

"Yes, it is," Kilborn chortled. "I know that last project didn't work out like we thought. But I believe in forgiving and forgetting."

"Since when?" Luke asked.

"Since I decided to make you another business proposition. Anyway, I'm sure you're planning to write a book about your experience in captivity, right?"

"Yes I am," Luke said.

"Well, that's another reason why I'm calling. I hope you will seriously consider publishing with us. My company would like to make you a generous offer for the rights to publish your book."

"Generous? How generous?"

"We're talking a million-dollar advance. That doesn't include the movie rights."

Luke smiled. He didn't say anything for about twenty seconds, wanting to soak up the irony.

"Who is that?" Hayley asked.

Luke put his hand over the phone. "The guy who was responsible for sending me to Utah in the first place," he said. Then he put the phone back to his lips.

"Well, Jack, that is very generous. The thing of it is, I've received about five other offers since I got home and I'm in the process of sorting through them."

"Oh, I see," Kilborn said, somewhat dejectedly.

"Feel free to fax or e-mail me a proposal and I'll take a look at it. You never know what might happen."

"Two million."

"Excuse me?"

"We'll pay you three million as an advance. The whole country is abuzz over your story. It's going to be a *New York Times* bestseller."

"Well, Jack, there's going to be a lot in my book about the power of faith and the power of prayer, stuff like that. From what I recall, you're not a big fan of those things."

"I am now."

"Really?" Luke said, wondering if Kilborn had also experienced a miraculous change of heart.

"Absolutely. Prayer and faith are en vogue right now in the country. Books about stuff like that are selling like crazy."

Luke sighed. "By the way, how's your daughter?" he asked.

"Audrey? Oh, she's, um, well, on one of your Church missions in Denmark. I actually went to a Mormon church and heard her speak before she left."

"Jack, if you learn a little more about the Mormons, you might find that you like it."

Kilborn roared with laughter. "Let's not get carried away," he said. "Before I go, I have to ask one question."

"Shoot."

"How did you escape from those terrorists, anyway?"

"You'll just have to read the book, won't you?" Luke said. "Nice talking to you, Jack."

"Same to you, Luke."

Smiling, Luke hung up the phone and held Hayley in his arms.

"Don't tell me *he* made you an offer?" she asked.

"He did. You know, the way it looks, with the money we'll be making from this book, we'll be able to buy a big house with a big backyard. Before you know it, we'll be living the Mormon-American dream."

"We already are," Hayley replied. "We don't need a big house or a big back yard. We have everything we need right here."

"You're right," Luke said.

"Now all you have to do," Hayley said, "is write that book. Then we can schedule your fireside speaking circuit."

"Well, first, I'm going to have to buy a new laptop," Luke said. "That's what I'm doing first thing tomorrow."

"We're going with you," Hayley said. "I'm never letting you out of my sight again. What ever happened to your old laptop, anyway?"

"I guess you could say it got fried," Luke said.

34

Speculation reached a fevered pitch. The baby was a little more than six weeks old and members of the Helaman 6th Ward were dying to find out what the Mannings were going to name her.

When the day of the blessing arrived, Luke and Hayley wouldn't tell anyone—not even her parents—the name they had chosen.

It wasn't that they wanted to keep it a secret, but they thought it would be special to announce it in a sacrament meeting setting. They just weren't expecting all of the interest and intrigue. The more people asked them what the name was, the more they wanted to wait.

Despite the Church's stance on wagering, both the Relief Society and Elder's Quorum had organized pools to guess the baby's name. The winner received a reprieve from clean-up duty at the next ward Christmas party.

In a somewhat unusual move, the congregation stood to sing "The Spirit of God" for the opening hymn. For Luke, the hymn brought back memories of his final night in captivity. For ward members, it brought back fond memories of the vigils they had held on a regular basis. For the rest of their lives, they couldn't hear that hymn and not think of Luke.

Upon his return from captivity, people in the ward looked at him differently—no longer as a recent convert but as someone who had been through the refiner's fire. Someone who understood what it meant to endure to the end. Luke finally felt like he was truly one of them, without an asterisk. He was simply a member of The Church of Jesus Christ of Latter-day Saints.

Ben conducted the meeting and after making a few announcements, he invited Luke forward to give a name and a blessing to his daughter. "We're all dying to find out what that name is," Ben said.

Luke took the baby, clad in a white dress donated by Hayley's visiting teachers, in his arms and stood up at the front of the chapel. Hayley immediately started sobbing. Grit, other members of Hayley's family, Ben, and Brother Gruber also joined the circle. Though the baby was calm and still, the arms that held her began bouncing her gently up and down.

"Brethren," Luke said, "let's try not to make her seasick. Hayley wouldn't be happy if the baby spit up all over her dress."

A deacon held the microphone up for Luke to speak into.

Luke thought about how before his terrifying experience in Sudan, he would have been terrified to perform such a sacred ordinance. Not anymore. After all those months of confinement, praying for hours every day, saying a prayer to Heavenly Father came naturally.

"Our Heavenly Father," Luke began, "by the authority of the Melchizedek Priesthood, we present this special infant before Thee to receive a name. And the name that we have chosen for her is . . . *Esther Sheila Manning.*"

Sister Fidrych's cavernous mouth was agape. Nobody saw that name coming. The men in the circle opened their eyes briefly and looked at Luke strangely. Everyone in the ward had lost the baby name pool sweepstakes. The closest was Stacie, who had correctly guessed Sheila, Luke's mom's name, as the middle name.

Luke offered a short but sweet blessing on his daughter.

"Esther, you are a precious daughter of a loving Heavenly Father," he said. "You have been well-prepared to come to Earth at this time. We love you so much and are so happy that you have joined our family. You have a special gift for bringing happiness into the lives of others. As you grow, stay close to your mom. Follow her example and learn from her. If you do, I promise you that you will be the type of woman our Father in Heaven expects you to be . . ."

When he was finished, he closed in the name of Jesus Christ. As he was walking back to his seat, Ben grabbed his arm.

"This is one of those silly Mormon traditions," Ben whispered, "but could you lift little Esther up so everyone can see her?"

Luke looked at Ben strangely, but did what he said. He looked out in the congregation and saw nothing but smiling faces. When he sat down next to Hayley, who was wiping the mascara from her cheeks, she took the baby.

"That was the best blessing I've ever heard," Hayley said to Luke.

"Thanks."

Brother Woodard, like everyone else, was perplexed. He was trying to get used to the fact that Esther was the name of his granddaughter. The only place he had ever heard of someone being named Esther—besides on his four-generational genealogical charts and barnyard animals—was in the Old Testament. So he opened up his Bible Dictionary to learn more about the name.

Esther, Book of. . . . The story belongs to the time of the Captivity . . . Esther, adopted daughter of Mordecai the Jew, was chosen as [the queen's] successor, on account of her beauty. Haman, chief man at the king's court, hated Mordecai, and having cast lots to find a suitable day, obtained a decree to put all Jews to death. Esther, at great personal risk, revealed her own nationality and obtained a reversal of the decree. It was decided that two days of feasting should be annually observed in honor of this deliverance . . . The book has no direct reference to God, but he is everywhere taken for granted, as the book infers a providential destiny and speaks of fasting for deliverance. There have been doubts at times as to whether it should be admitted to the canon of scripture. But the book has a religious value as containing a most striking illustration of God's overruling providence in history, and as exhibiting a very high type of courage, loyalty, and patriotism.

Throughout the rest of the meetings, ward members were talking about the name, making sure they were out of the earshot of Luke and Hayley.

"Esther? Why Esther? That's the name of an 80-year-old spinster. That poor girl. Such a strange name for a beautiful baby."

"Well, we can't judge them too harshly. Both Luke and Hayley have been under a lot of stress the past nine months."

"What kind of a name is Esther?"

"Hebrew, I think."

After church, Hayley's family showed up at the Manning house for the obligatory post-blessing get-together, complete with ham, potatoes, veggie trays, and fruit punch.

Grit noticed a book of baby names sitting on the kitchen table. He picked it up and read that Esther was a Hebrew name that meant "star."

After grabbing a handful of cherry tomatoes, Grit cornered Luke. "You did a fine job today," he said.

"Thanks," Luke replied.

"And we love the name you've picked for our granddaughter," Grit added.

"Really?" Luke asked, knowing people would be shocked by the name they had chosen. It wasn't exactly common. It wasn't a name he would have ever imagined giving to a pet, let alone a child.

"I have to hand it to you. You and Hayley really did your homework in choosing the name."

"What do you mean?" Luke asked.

"I just read all the background about Esther in the Old Testament and read what the name means," Grit said. "And it fits her perfectly, I think."

"Hmmmm," Luke said. "I didn't even know there was an Esther in the Bible. I guess I'll have to read it."

"If you didn't know that name from the Bible, then where did you come up with it?" Grit asked.

"It's the name of someone I met in Sudan," Luke said. "Don't worry. I'll explain it all in my book."

"Luke," called Hayley, who was dishing up some mint brownies, "I think I heard Esther crying. Would you mind checking on her?"

Though Luke couldn't hear a thing, he did what he was

asked. "I'd love to," he said. Then he turned to Grit. "Excuse me. Duty calls."

"I told you that you'd make a wonderful dad," Grit said, smiling.

Luke approached the bedroom and, sure enough, Esther was fussing.

"Your mom must have bionic hearing," he said to her.

Luke picked Esther up in his arms and she stopped crying right away. He gazed past those long eyelashes and into those puppy-dog eyes. He stroked her auburn hair.

"You saved my life," he said to her. "Without you and Brooklyn, I never would have survived. I'm going to spend the rest of my life paying you back for what you did for me and your mom. I can't wait to play catch with you and take you to ballgames. But we'll give you a few months before we start that stuff."

He sat down in the customized rocking chair that Brother Gruber had made for Hayley and the baby, then slowly rocked her to sleep.

Luke kissed Esther on the cheek and whispered in her tiny ear: "I love you forever."

THE END

ABOUT THE AUTHOR

Jeff Call lives in Cedar Hills, Utah, with his wife, CherRon, and their six sons. He served an LDS mission to Chile and later graduated with a bachelor's degree in journalism from BYU. Jeff is a sports reporter for *The Deseret Morning News*.

Return to Mormonville: Worlds Apart is the sequel to his first novel, *Mormonville*. He is also the author of *Rolling With The Tide*.

The author can be reached via e-mail at:
jeff_call_2000@yahoo.com

9 26575 77999 1